The Ice Carriers

by the Author

The Masterpiece
The Secret
The Injury

Anna Enquist

The Ice Carriers

TRANSLATED BY

Jeannette K. Ringold

The Toby Press

First English Language Edition 2003

The Toby Press LLC
www.tobypress.com

Originally published as *De IJsdragers*

ISBN 1 902881 78 8

A CIP catalogue record for this title is available from the British Library

Typeset in Garamond by Jerusalem Typesetting

Printed and bound in the United States by Thomson-Shore Inc., Michigan

I dedicate this book to my daughter, Margit,
who, with her literary knowledge and her great sensitivity,
helped me to complete it.

Chapter one

Sandy soil was something she had always hated, even though many people spoke highly of it. It was supposed to be good for the skin and healthy for the lungs. She detested the nonchalantly swept up dunes with their nasty beach grass. She despised the element that let itself be spread so easily by the wind, that so powerlessly let the saving rain seep through it and that lent itself so uncritically for use as an abrasive or a timepiece. As a child, she would stand on the beach and watch how the wind drove enormous streams of sand before it, about four inches above the ground; she felt the grains sting against her calves and laughed. Pointless excitement, childish force.

Nico said that they lived splendidly here. That many people would envy them this old-fashioned, spacious house, surrounded by a good-sized piece of land on the edge of the dunes. It didn't occur to him that not much would grow in this soil; it escaped his notice that she'd had cartloads of black soil and countless bags of dried cow manure dumped only to have it disappear into the ground. The result was a modest patch of grass in the middle of the garden. Beyond it, the sand had already crept back up, searching for heather and pine trees, dry companions of the dune landscape.

She loved polders. Clay, lush grass, and lots of water. There, a rise of the land served a purpose, gave structure and meaning. Dikes referred to rivers, and fences marked the paths. For the rest, everything was smooth, flat and orderly; the grassland was crisscrossed in a comprehensible way by narrow ditches and was green all the way to the horizon. And then toward evening a skein of geese alighted on the nutritious soccer field: the birds cut the grass with their saw-toothed bills, contentedly stuck their heads under a wing and slept. No nervous beating of the waves but restful waters.

She had to take the groceries out of the car and put them away before Nico came home. The sun hung above the dark coniferous wood. She took off her shoes and her socks and walked barefoot on her artificial paradise of grass. It was drying out at the edges, she noticed.

She had parked the car in such a way that there was plenty of space for Nico's Saab. She would put his non-alcoholic beer in the refrigerator, the lamb, the lettuce. The soles of her feet arched above the pebbles of the driveway. The trunk popped open and showed off a profusion of plants: tomatoes, zucchinis, pumpkins. She lugged them to the area that she had designated as vegetable garden, as far away as possible from the dark trees. To be ready, she placed a shovel and a sack of garden soil near it. Perhaps this evening, if not, then tomorrow morning before she left for school. The first two hours she had the intermediate level, but they had a study week. Enough time.

Slowly and carefully she organized the refrigerator, and while she was doing that, she heard his car drive up the road. She washed her hands under the kitchen faucet, forced her shoulders down, and walked into the hall.

Before Nico could put his key into the lock, she pulled the door open for him. He placed his heavy briefcase against the wall and kissed her hair in passing, on the way to the kitchen, to the bottle of gin.

"One drink," he said, and after that he would drink harmless beer in order to be clear-headed for this evening's meeting.

What could she say? How was your day; are you in the mood for lamb chops; what is the meeting about; what time do you have to leave? Silently she followed him to the kitchen. He had taken off his jacket and had hung it over a chair. He squeezed the lettuce that lay on the countertop, took the bottle from the refrigerator and sat down at the table, his legs wide apart.

"You want some too?" He filled his glass and lifted it to his mouth, sighing. She waited until she heard him swallow and exhaled, as intently as you would watch a child putting away a mouthful of food.

"Yes, go ahead," she said. When she sat down across from him he smiled. He rubbed his face with both hands.

He needs a haircut, she thought; his hair hangs over his collar. He looks sweet, a little scruffy; I prefer him like that rather than with his hair trimmed. The shine is gone, he's tired. I will right away, in a minute, shortly, soon, make dinner for him. She saw in her mind how she would tear the lettuce, how she would cut the tomatoes and the onion, first in a check pattern and then straight across into small pieces; she would get out the goat cheese and the delicious oil that she'd bought recently. Meanwhile, he was talking. What was it about? Words that flowed over the kitchen table and slid to the floor like syrup. She looked at her bare feet below the jeans. Socks? Oh yes, on the grass.

"They want to have that service but not pay for it. They're unleashing a lot of resistance; they're letting all sorts of drifters and social educators get together without intervening. Incitement!"

He leaned back and saw how she got up, pulled out the knife and cutting board, bent forward to the vegetable bin.

"At eight o'clock in the city hall with the police and a city council member. I'll have to give them some bad news. Beautiful, certainly, such a crisis center, but it costs us eight expensive full-time workers who just sit and twiddle their thumbs all day long among the empty beds, in addition to bonuses for irregular hours. Hein Bruggink calculated it for me; you could keep half a department going for that money. Nice blouse you're wearing."

Spring onions, they're delicious. Carefully cut the parsley over it with scissors. Olives, fresh thyme.

"Hein says that it's the city council's problem. We would like it but can't afford it. I have to get them to solve it. And offer alternatives."

She placed the dishes and the bowl with salad on the table, rubbed the silver with a dishtowel, took wineglasses from the cupboard.

"You can have people come to the emergency room of a regular hospital, or to the police station. A higher threshold, less expertise up front, but with good backup from us—it makes sense. I'd rather have beer."

Another glass. An opener. Pour it. The lamb sizzles in the pan. Now there was shade in the garden; she saw her shoes lying on the dark grass—one was still standing up straight, the other was lying on its side a bit farther away.

She loaded the dishwasher and he rummaged in his study at the front of the house to gather his papers. It was seven-thirty, the sun was gone, and the air was becoming hazy. Suddenly he was behind her, massaging her shoulders. She turned around quickly, waved him away with a joke, and watched him as he walked to the car waving with his file.

Her feet slid into the wooden clogs that stood next to the kitchen door. She placed the spade perpendicularly on the soil and pushed it into the ground. She dug deep into the sand, a wide hole. The thick plastic of the bag with soil wouldn't break; she placed the sack down flat and hacked a cross into it with the spade. Now she could fling soil into the hole with both hands; finally she placed a pumpkin plant with lots of buds into the fertile circle. Next one.

Hurrying, she continued working in the twilight. Because she kept wiping her hair out of her face, soil was sticking on her nose and forehead. She sweated and breathed heavily through her mouth.

When she stopped for a moment, leaning on the spade with one hand and pushing the other one against her back, she saw a woman standing on the balcony of the house next door. She gave a quick wave and bent back over the soil.

Get back inside, you prying bitch. Plants have to go into the soil right away, otherwise they'll dry out. Or: you should never plant during the day, it exhausts the plants; night is best. The first water should be dew. Or: my day is so full, my job so busy, my work so important, that I can only take care of my plants in the evening. Maybe one of those plaid skirts will grow from my waist if I live here long enough.

The last tomato plant was in its place. She kicked off her clogs and, dragging her feet over the grass, walked to the garden hose. Around each plant she created a mud puddle, after that she rinsed her hands with the ice-cold water.

Dead tired she got into bed. She had to set the alarm a bit earlier because she hadn't managed to go over the stack of translation tests. She had unpacked her bag, laid out books and papers on the big table, reached in the bookcase behind her for the dictionary and commentary, and started as she usually did. When she'd reached the homework of the third pupil she felt bogged down; she couldn't concentrate and felt her eyes sting and her eyelids become heavy.

Sleep came quickly. Only once did she drift to the surface before losing consciousness, fearful and startled by something she didn't know, but when she turned with her face to the window she could let herself go.

She woke up when Nico lay down next to her.

"Success," he said softly, "the crisis center will be abolished in six weeks. It was too much for them. A victory!"

She was immediately alert.

"But you lost. Didn't you really want that center, didn't you like it?"

She heard that her voice sounded high and nagging.

"Yes, but they should have helped to pay. We are a psychiatric hospital; we can't just play soup kitchen and crisis center. It was an experiment that didn't work. I'm glad I could put an end to it."

He tossed and turned until he was comfortable, with his hand on her hip. She looked at the gray square of the window, behind which the austere conifers stood against the dark sky. It took a long time, too long, before she said anything. Nico was already breathing deeply and regularly.

"If someone doesn't know where to go, is confused or in a panic—if someone is afraid of psychiatrists or doesn't dare to go to an institution—aren't they glad to have the crisis center? Then there's a place in the middle of the city where someone can go who's at the end of his rope. Even at night."

Nico sighed. He caressed her head until his fingers touched her wet cheeks. Then he turned over and pulled up his knees.

*

When she came out of school the weather was still glorious. She felt energetic, competent, contented. That morning the new plants had been standing proud and erect in their deep-black beds; the students had listened attentively when she handed out the translation tests with kind but objective comments; above the canals hung a saturated, warm light.

She wanted to go and have a quick look at the herbs in the flower market, but she remained standing in the shadow of the houses on the large square. Actually she didn't feel like lugging shopping bags and plastic bags with plants in them, and preferred to drink a beer on this half-empty terrace, in the pleasant warmth of the afternoon sun.

She stretched her legs and looked through her eyelashes at the façade of the church across the way. Vaguely she heard two women talking to each other about summer clothes, whether or not to wear stockings, an engagement, that is if Hein can come. She opened her eyes and saw a sturdy woman bicycle away with a sports bag on her handlebars. The other, blonde, perfectly groomed, dressed in a light yellow suit, was standing in front of her with a tennis racket under her arm, and smiling at her.

She tried as swiftly as possible to figure out who it was. She felt that she knew. Not a colleague from school. Not one of Nico's staff members. Someone with status; the wife of the lawyer, the family doctor? No: Ineke Tordoir, the wife of Albert, the chairman of Nico's Board of Trustees. The fact that she'd pinpointed the woman's name and function made her smile with relief—which the other interpreted as a sign to approach.

"Louise! How nice. I'll come and sit down with you!" The woman let her eyes slide over her checked blouse, her jeans, and the glass of beer; she ordered water.

"You must be coming from your work. I admire you so much for your work with those unruly children—and a difficult subject—French, wasn't it? A wonderful language if you can manage it!"

"Classical languages," she muttered. The other just kept on talking as if a sound source had been turned on that was impossible to turn off.

"I can't imagine being among those adolescents all day long. I'm so happy that both my sons are past that phase. They're both in Delft now; I don't think they study a lot, but they're having a good time. Sometimes I think that I should go back to work again too, but then it gets so hectic that nothing comes of it. Albert is so terribly busy that everything falls on my shoulders. Of course he's already swamped by the court, and then something like the hospital is added to it! That business about the crisis center—he has been called in to account for it. He has to have a meeting with the health insurance provider or with the employee-management council, or God knows what. No, I don't think I'll get a job again."

The blonde woman tapped the steel of her racket and smiled at her amiably. The make-up lay evenly on her perfect skin. Two sons in Delft, fat, tiresome boys who had attended Louise's school, but classical civilization had been wasted on them. What kind of work would such a woman have done? She couldn't imagine anything.

"Nico must be working day and night too, right? Of course it's stressful, but Albert's obligations are different. He has in fact complete political responsibility. A decision like that is difficult these days with all those homeless and disturbed types who hang around. I think that there's always something with that hospital—Albert has many worries about it. And then, on top of it all, there's Hein Bruggink who's going to retire. Parties, farewell speeches, and the question of succession of course. No, it could be a little less hectic—we're never at home together in the evening."

She registered that last comment with surprise. Just like Nico not to say anything about the departure of his director before it was clear how things would go. No surprises and above all no expectations where the outcome would be unclear. Surely he was not looking forward to getting a new boss, or a number of bosses. These days it was called a Board of Directors. Actually, he found his position as physician-in-chief to his liking; he made policy on a practical level; he had a lot of contact with colleagues and also saw patients once in a while. He wouldn't want to change that. Don't let that woman notice that I didn't know. She drank her beer and remained silent.

"Your husband has an equally responsible job," Ineke rattled on. "I think that men burden you so much, you know, the way they always run on when they come home, about one meeting or the other or some policy consultation. I think that it really saps your energy as a wife. Is it easy for you to summon that? Fortunately your children are out of the house too, aren't they? Didn't you have a daughter? Must have left home by now? Is she doing something interesting?"

Just as I explained to my Latin class this afternoon: register it without expression or reaction, just as Tacitus did. I see the pink mouth move over the shiny teeth; from the nostrils to the corners of the upper lip two wrinkles pull and make the cheeks round; the penciled eyebrows are raised when the eyes open wide. Without expression or reaction. She picked up her bag, shook the woman's hand and walked away—straight across the square, in a straight line.

The upper floor was a lot smaller than the ground floor; that was because of the straw roof that tapered. Yet their bedroom with the balcony was enormous, and the adjacent bathroom was a good-sized one, too. She bent over the washbasin and looked at herself in the mirror. Through the open door she saw the landing behind her, the beginning of the wooden stairs with their wide low treads, and the closed door of the third room.

Turn it into your study, Nico had said. You need space for your books; you have to be able to sit somewhere quietly to prepare classes and grade papers. Later, she had answered. Later. She splashed cold water against her face. Back downstairs she unpacked her bag in the living room, looked in her pocket calendar, and made stacks of the various things she had to do: Ovid with the fourth period, a mythology lesson for the first period, a list of Greek prepositions for the third period. She had to have control, modest short-term plans, tasks that would keep her occupied. She walked into the garden and sat down on the edge of the terrace. The impertinence of that woman, such indiscretion! Actually she hadn't been unpleasant, she meant well. Stupid of Albert, he should never have mentioned the director's departure before it was officially announced. He should have taken into account his wife's talkativeness—after so many years of marriage he should have known that. No expression, she said to herself. What was going to happen in the hospital didn't really interest her at all. That other thing, something else the woman had said—it had caused agitation, a gnawing feeling in her stomach, a dull, apathetic fatigue. She would rather count the blades of grass at her feet than reflect. All thoughts stopped in front of that closed door on the upper floor, certainly when Nico was home. At moments like now, with a certain distance, she herself could formulate a thought like: There is a daughter whom we don't know. We haven't heard from her for more than half a year and we don't know where she is. Her room is empty. On her birthday I lay in bed all day, sick with a headache. She had turned nineteen. Nico went bicycling and came home with a cut on his knee. Fallen. Bicycle smashed.

She felt other thoughts pushing aside the main line of thought. What dinner should be this evening, how many weeks until Easter vacation, had she hung the laundry, what she would do with that dull area in the garden near the pine trees. That she should get a gardener to help her with that hopeless soil.

During the conversation with the woman she had briefly been tempted to tell her everything. A daughter, yes, her name is Maj, after my mother who is from Sweden. A solitary child with a frown on her forehead and a frightened look in her eyes. She ran away right before her final examination. My husband doesn't want to talk about her. We act as if she doesn't exist, but she is there—she is there all the time.

People say that disasters become easier to handle if you talk about them, but unfortunately we don't have that experience.

The round, smooth face of the woman had frightened her off. Even if she had really wanted to, she wouldn't have been able to get a word in. Maybe. I have to go, she had said when she managed to get her lips unstuck: I've suddenly remembered I have an appointment.

"I saw Albert's wife in the city. At first I couldn't remember who she was. She plays tennis with Aleid Bruggink. Her name is Ineke; fortunately it came to me just in time."

Nico looked up from his paper.

"You *talked* with her?"

"She can't be stopped, I had to. But I didn't have to say anything, she did the talking. She sat down by me on a terrace!"

Nico folded the paper.

"They want to live in France, in that house where we are always welcome but where we never go. He's been considering it for a while. I think that he's just about done what he had planned in the hospital. It's quiet now, except for the crisis center. He probably doesn't feel like being part of the next round of negotiations about cutbacks. Hein always wants to come out ahead."

Now I should say it, she thought. A comment about the two fat sons in Delft, and how that made me think of Maj. Couldn't we call in a private investigator, place ads in the paper, go by her friends one more time?

"Don't look so gloomy," said Nico.

He pulled her up and pressed her against him. She felt the weight of his arms, his breath in her hair. As if he's consoling me, she thought, as if he knows what I'm thinking and is with me. He doesn't know that at all, he doesn't console me, and yet I feel it as such because I want to. If I don't do that, I won't have anything at all.

They bicycled into the city to eat in the market square. Where the dunes became meadows, a purple light lay on the fields. In the outskirts, children were playing in the street; as they bicycled past, a boy clutched a ball with both hands under his chin, halting his movements, freezing time for a moment until they had passed.

It was too cold to sit outside, but the space of the square seemed to give the inside room extra style and more air. They clinked glasses filled with cool wine. Nico waved at a serious man with neatly combed hair who answered the greeting with a solemn nod.

"Te Velde, from financial administration. What's he doing here by himself? Maybe he's waiting for someone."

For his daughter, she thought when she saw a thin girl with a violin case come through the revolving door and look searchingly around the room. Nico talked about the hospital, the demands made by the administrators, interference from the Ministry, the necessity of doing your own research, quality control, individualized care, rehabilitation programs.

She had difficulty concentrating on his words. What was it all supposed to mean? For her these were abstract and vague concepts. For him it was different: his face flushed, his voice filled with passion.

Formerly, when he was a resident, he would captivate her with his psychiatric stories about people with strange behaviors and bizarre thoughts. Then it was important to understand what was going on inside a patient. She'd always found it touching, a group of students and residents sitting in a circle around a professor and trying, through their own associations, to discover the meaning of cries of despair carefully recorded in files. Nico had hated it. He couldn't do it. His preliminary psychiatry test had been a disaster. The professor, a slightly effeminate artistic man, had leaned back in his chair with half-closed eyes and had placed a rose in a milk bottle on the table in front of Nico.

"Tell me about this rose, Mr. Van der Doelen. I'm listening."

Nico hadn't known what he should say. His thinking had become completely blocked, even his blood circulation seemed to falter—there was no movement anywhere. The professor had smiled ironically.

"Numerous writers and poets have preceded you, Mr. Van der Doelen. With your knowledge of the soul you must have something to add to their reflections."

Silence. Pearls of sweat on his forehead. Paralysis.

"If you can't say anything about this simple flower, with its clearly visible ambivalence of razor-sharp thorns and velvet flower petals, if you can't formulate any thoughts about the concealed heart and the thirsty stem—how can I possibly unleash you on my patients? A psychiatric patient is much more complicated than this rose, Mr. Van der Doelen. We'll meet again in three months. In the meantime, do try to do some reflecting."

He'd been furious, and stuttering with rage he had told her the story—beside himself with indignation. How humiliating, she had thought. He had been made to look ridiculous, been made a fool of, emasculated. Before the re-examination period expired, the professor had become ill. Nico did a brilliant examination with his replacement who specialized in directive therapy and structuring techniques.

Yet, sometimes she thought he'd been right, that poetic professor. Someone with a mental illness was probably served better by a person who tried to reconstruct his story, than by an imposed schedule with rules. Someone who was confused didn't understand himself; in which case it was good if others did their best to summon their understanding. If a doctor doesn't dare to be curious about the nature of the patient, how can the patient ever dare to look at himself? How dreadful for the sick person to get a sheet filled with behavioral exercises with the implicit message that the people giving treatment didn't care how the patient is put together and why he had ended up there. She still thought, as she did then, that the sick person should be viewed like the rose, with wonder, with concern, with understanding. But what did she know? It wasn't her field. Nico talked about the chaos that you had to contain, about clear rules and agreements, about reward for adaptation, and punishment for transgression. And the correcting influence of the group. Someone who was really sick didn't get better from a free-floating search for meaning; it was better not to look a paranoid patient in the eyes because that only made it worse; you shouldn't keep asking about strange pronouncements, but should extinguish them by ignoring them.

She looked at the man who sat across from her. His plate was empty, but he continued to hold knife and fork at the ready, as if they were tools with which he could attack reality. She smiled. He put down his fork and took her hand.

"I've come to a decision," he said.

She looked at him, surprised, in spite of herself thinking of a definite search for their daughter, of solving their own family mystery with the same energetic attention that was now being given to the hospital—and stopped herself immediately. He wasn't like that.

"I'm going to succeed Hein. I'll become director."

Chapter two

When he became physician-in-chief, he got a room in the main building. That was convenient because everyone could find him there and he was at the center of decision-making and administration. But he missed the bustle of a ward in the background, the slightly too loud and jovial voices of the nurses, the shuffling patients in the hall. He noticed only now that he seemed to be attached to it after all—or was he simply afraid to lose his real profession? He hadn't been that happy with the almost daily disputes between psychiatrists and the nursing staff, with the difficult task of bringing about a more or less safe and pleasant social climate on a ward where new and seriously disturbed people continually had to find a place—yet he thrived with each crisis. Decisions to isolate or knock a patient out with sedatives, to reprimand a resident or to transfer a nurse cost him no difficulty; on the contrary, he liked overseeing chaos, making decisions at lightning speed, and carrying them out firmly. He thought that looking for a new balance afterwards was boring and tedious. It took too long for him, everyone had to have a say, with objections and obstacles, so that decisions were weakened or turned back.

He had been surprised at the offer of a promotion and hadn't thought about it long, had accepted!

Now he made decisions about preferred medications and treatment protocols, made final decisions when others couldn't do it, and steered the colossal ship that was the hospital in a direction that he himself had chosen, within the economic boundaries set up by Bruggink, but still.

He placed his bag on his desk and immediately walked back out of the building. The grounds looked like a sleepy and very rural village. Tall trees stood along the paths, and the buildings lay hidden among the green. On the roads walked a person carrying papers under his arm, chugged a cart with garden tools, shuffled a group of patients. Everyone said hello. In the distance a train went by. Between the railway and the hospital grounds there was a fence ten-foot high. There, at the far end of the grounds, was the pavilion where he was going.

He himself still thought of it as the "chronic ward," but in current usage it was at most called the "residential pavilion," a word that eliminated the endless, hopeless aspect—after all, you could stay somewhere without it being forever. In practice this was the case, for the people who were admitted there almost never left again. In the course of the years, the length of stay in the "acute" wards had become ever shorter; here an atmosphere of decisiveness, of objectives and designated levels of treatment dominated, and whoever couldn't keep up became chronic. Because of this, the hospital clogged up slowly, a problem that demanded his attention.

He opened the door of the ancient and dilapidated building with his own key and was met by the smell of tobacco and stale coffee. From the living room came accordion music. A sturdily built male nurse in a short-sleeved shirt was steering a number of patients from the hall into the room. Nico glanced into the ward: fluttering sheets, piles of dirty linen on the floor, an open window that looked out at a fence, people in the two farthest beds. In the living room, rumpled patients were sitting round a table with coffee cups. People spilled tobacco, ashes, cookie crumbs. A woman had put her arms on the table and was sleeping. A stale, sour smell hung in the air. He sat down in the office with a stack of patient files. The inside window gave him a full view of the living room where a young woman was hanging streamers. Between her lips she pressed a row of thumbtacks; she had a mouth tight with metal. In the corners of the room she climbed on a chair and attached a string with small colored pennants against the molding; in doing this she tightened her gluteus for a moment.

He heard a nurse screaming in the ward: "Get up, you've been warned three times! We're going to pull you out of bed—it's Mrs. Van Overeem's birthday!"

On the table, in front of the sleeping woman, Nico saw a cardboard box with chocolate napoleons. Alongside the back wall of the room a young man was walking back and forth nervously, continually casting hurried glances at the pastries.

"You have to come and sit down too, Johan," said the nurse, "we're having a party, everyone has to sit at the table."

He pulled an old man with a drawn-in mouth to the table in his wheelchair. The man clutched a cigar butt in his hand and asked for a light.

"With the coffee," the nurse shouted. "When everyone is finally seated I'll get you matches. Come, Johan!"

The young man took three steps toward the table, snatched away the metal teapot with tulips in it and flung it with full force through the window. He was immediately grabbed and pulled into the hall by the bare-armed man and a woman who rushed up.

"Back to number two?" she asked, panting.

The isolation cells were at the end of the hall. Bent over his case histories, Nico listened to the vehement dragging and shuffling, accompanied by the shrill screaming of the young man.

In the living room, the young woman swept up the shattered glass with a dustpan and brush. What a chaos it was in there, Nico thought. In the corner stood broken chairs, dead plants in chipped pots; stacks of old magazines and messy boxes with puzzles lay on the windowsill.

The patients remained sitting around the table. Some moved

their upper bodies back and forth; others sat and stared straight ahead.

"Where is the coffee?" shouted the woman who was lying across the table, without lifting her head. "Coffee, coffee, coffee!!"

The man with the bare arms and his colleague returned to the room. Violent pounding could be heard from the isolation cell.

What a shambles, what a bleak setting. Stinking wards, noise everywhere, a racket, too little space, which in addition was filled with broken junk. The worst was perhaps the total apathy of the inhabitants. This was their life, and, except for the locked-up young man, they accepted it.

The young woman handed out napoleons on paper plates. Slowly, one of the patients was squeezing the hard tops and bottoms together; the thick, yellowish cream dripped into her lap. A nurse walked toward her, took a deep breath, and saw Nico sitting in the office. She exhaled, as if she were deflating and collapsing. With a dishcloth she dabbed up the muck.

The man with the bare arms came to ask if he wanted coffee too. Nico declined the offer.

"Shouldn't a psychiatrist be checking on the isolation cell?" he asked.

"He's off sick," said the man. "And there's no substitute. We can handle it ourselves—plenty of experience here. Or do you want to take a look yourself? Not such a good idea—he doesn't know you. Wouldn't you like a napoleon?"

In the garden room, the young woman started to sing. "Happy birthday to you! Happy birthday to you!" No one sang along.

"Hip, hip hurrah," she sang softly in conclusion. She blushed deeply.

Finally there was quiet around the table. The patients were being fed or ate by themselves the pastry that had been cut into small squares. The sleeping woman lifted her head and saw Nico sitting in the office.

"Hallelujah! Doctor Van der Doelen has come! Amen!" She

called out in a singsong voice. She let her face drop into the pastry and spread her arms out over the table.

"There's a strange smell here," said the young woman, "as if something is smoldering; is there anything on the stove, Erik?"

The man with the bare arms shook his head, and started to examine the room carefully. Now Nico smelled it too, a nasty burning smell with a synthetic undertone. The whole mess here should actually burn down, he thought. Relief, insurance money, new building.

Shaking his head Erik came back from the kitchen, his nostrils flared and eyes half-closed, following the scent. He pointed to the wheelchair, which was turned halfway to the corner. A small, dirty yellow wisp of smoke was rising from it. Erik reached to the table where the teapot with flowers had stood and threw himself onto the wheelchair. The young woman had run to the kitchen and returned with a bottle of milk, which she emptied into the lap of the wheelchair occupant. The man's face revealed nothing. He sat. He looked. He was silent. Erik pushed him onto his side and pulled half a cigar out of his trouser pocket. Carefully he picked at the fabric that was burned to bits on the thighs and uncovered a bright red, blistering wound. Trying to comfort him, the young woman caressed the head of the old man, who continued to stare ahead undisturbed.

Nico stood up, put away the case history reports, and with determined strides left the pavilion.

*

From the church building in the middle of the grounds came fragments of song. He walked in without thinking. He felt irritated, impatient, restless. Walking over the sandy paths he had started sweating, now the cold of the church hit his damp skin. He leaned against the wall next to the entrance and looked into the dark space. Here, too, there was an enormous mess: stacked church benches, brooms thrown in a corner, buckets, mops, a rack with drums and triangles, open music cupboards, psalters dumped on the floor.

In the middle of the room, under the clerestory that let the sun through in dusty rays, stood the Hospital Choir, a shabby group of twenty, consisting mainly of patients, but supplemented by staff. The conductor, a heavy man with curly hair, clasped a recorder in his left hand and had fastened a drum around his waist with a belt. He gestured exaggeratedly with his arms and hopped at the heavy beats.

What amateurism, what misplaced cheerfulness, what abject misery, Nico thought. Choral singing. And those managers and nurses are participating too. On the back row he even saw one of the psychiatrists, a serious woman with large hands. They give up their lunch break to suck up dust in here—unbelievable.

Disgusted, he made a move to go back outside but stopped when the choir broke into a new song: "I say adieu, we two, we have to part …"

The clear baritone of the conductor could be heard above the hesitating voices of the choir. A farewell song for Bruggink, of course. The simple melody, with its recurring melancholic phrases, held him. The poignant song, first carried by the staff members but gradually joined more confidently by the whole choir and accompanied by the drum, possessed him from top to toe.

We are all imprisoned within the gates of these grounds, he thought, within the web of agreements that we have made about illness and cure; we barely know the illusions we depend on; we are completely powerless but we will collapse when that dawns on us—the caregivers as well as those cared for. Their voices spiral around one another, they sing words: joy and pain, adieu, parting, I will always be with you.

His thoughts made him miserable. He straightened his back, shook his head, and felt how his feet had contact with the floor. Powerlessness is a useless feeling; it paralyzes and makes you depressed. Away with it! Get outside, take action.

On the steps he met the young woman arm in arm with an old lady. He held the door open for her and when she passed, he smelled a strange, wild perfume that surprised him.

"How is Mr. Van Raai?" he asked when she was almost inside.

She looked around, the blond hair sliding on her shoulders. She had gray eyes.

"He was taken to the hospital by ambulance. It was much worse than we thought. It seemed as if he didn't feel any pain. I don't understand it."

"Have you worked here for a long time?"

"Two weeks. I'm a substitute. A student. Eva Passchier."

"Nico Van der Doelen." He shook the hand that she'd extended towards him, a hand which felt dry and cool. Crazy that they let a child like that mess around on that ward. How old is she anyway?

"Adieu, we two have to part, adieu, adieu," sang the choir. Eva took the lady by the arm and went inside.

*

The farewell to Hein Bruggink lasted for weeks. There was an enormous reception for the staff; there was a dinner with the Board of Trustees, a big party for all the patients, and a two-day conference about psychiatry and architecture for the psychiatrists and the managers. Nico had no patience to listen to the lectures; he could figure out himself that the form of the buildings had an influence on the nature of the treatment. Or the other way round. He decided to appear only at the dinner. In the afternoons, as the only psychiatrist in the hospital, he felt like a general and king. He walked from one department to the other; it was more or less quiet everywhere, which gave him the chance to reflect on his plans. In his imagination he combined pavilions, dismissed incompetent employees, and developed treatment protocols for patients who were considered unmanageable. New spearheads; cut fearlessly into rotten meat; make choices without looking back. These flights of the imagination intoxicated him, and when in the late afternoon he saw Eva sitting on a bench under a tree, he stopped in front of her to tell her what occupied his mind.

"These people you're looking after haven't had any responsibility for their own existence for twenty or thirty years. You determine their daily schedule, you figure out what they eat and when and where. They no longer have to do anything, they don't even have to want anything!"

The sneakers on her dangling legs wore two grooves in the sand. The sun shone on her bent neck.

"It's true," she said looking up. "I asked Mr. Van Raai this morning if he wanted to sit in the corner or at the table. He didn't know. Erik said: 'At the table.'"

"Choices!" shouted Nico. "Making choices means taking on responsibility, giving form to your own existence, being someone!"

She had perfect ankles. Tanned brown and naked, the instep disappeared into her shoe.

He walked on. He would abolish the Therapeutic Community, TC as it was called here; that was a lost cause from the seventies, a high-priced undertaking where relatively well-integrated patients sat digging into their souls for months, under the guidance of highly-trained therapists. The money made available would be spent on the most hopeless group in his care. As soon as Hein was gone.

The hotel where the conference was being held was on the sea. The sun shone red into his eyes when he turned into the parking lot. He felt tired and remained seated for a moment with his hands in his lap. Suddenly it was unthinkable to mingle cheerfully among his colleagues, to listen to the umpteenth farewell speech for Bruggink, to watch the behavior of the managers who wanted to impress. Dead weight hung on his shoes when he got out. On an impulse he ran down the stairs to the beach. On the sand he took off his shoes and socks. He rolled up his trousers and started running along the shore. At first he was bothered by the wallet and car keys in the pockets of his jacket, but he soon banished them from his thoughts. His bare feet smacked on the wet sand and steering clear of washed ashore jellyfish and glass demanded his complete attention. He forced himself to go at a tempo just beyond the threshold of his stamina and abandoned himself to the pace he had set.

Wait. Talk with Albert. Present his plan during a meeting of the Board of Trustees. Sit down at the short side of the table. Explain that he couldn't function in a Board of Directors as part of a fashionable troika or even worse, a duo. He wanted to be the only one responsible and therefore had to become the only director. That was cheaper too. With a good team under him, of course. Make good time. Win over the organization. An adventure for employees and patients. Take command. Concentration.

A dog danced along the tide line. Time after time, a child threw a piece of driftwood into the surf, and the animal threw himself in after it, dove in, barked, shook itself, was frightened by the waves rolling in, but continued to search until he could bring his prize onto the beach. The child kneeled, spreading its arms.

He saw it was a girl, about ten years old. She pressed the wet dog against her, stood up and waved the wood high above her head. The dog stood on his hind legs, barking.

He felt a stitch in his side, and just at that moment he stepped on the sharp edge of a shell. Cursing, he stopped, for the first time aware that the sand was cold and the sea was wet. He turned around and saw the hotel lying in the distance. The windows were already illuminated. He walked toward it at a calm pace. With difficulty he wriggled the socks over his wet feet. Sand. It was way up in his trousers, it stuck to his hair and made his eyes sting. He hauled himself up the stairs, conscious of the damp, turned-up trousers. The doorman watched him as he walked across the marble floor to the foyer.

From the spacious room came a constant rumble of conversation. Nico remained standing at the entrance and let his eyes travel over his colleagues who were standing together in small groups, drinking, joking and laughing. Here and there, strategically spread out, he saw members of the Board of Trustees, and in the farthest corner, near the large window that looked out over the sea, sat Hein Bruggink with a cigar.

He was a regent, an old-fashioned merchant, a superior trader. Under his leadership the hospital had gained economic health; he had spent his energy developing services and products that he resold, usually successfully. In his institutional kitchen meals were prepared that were purchased for miles around, his laundry served half the city, and in the nursing homes of the region his psychiatric expertise was purchased without stinting.

There would be an end to all that, Nico thought with sudden clarity. We have to become a hospital once again. Under my leadership. Out with trade, in with treatment.

He walked into the room, shook hands, accepted a drink, chatted with various people. He saw himself moving through the space. While engaged in this way, he observed his own progress along the various groups with great lucidity. He thought he was pleasant; he didn't begrudge Hein his last triumphal evening; he knew how he would carry out his own plan.

Hein's authoritarian, not very empathetic attitude had strangely enough made him popular with all levels of the staff. People saw Bruggink as a stern father, busy earning the family income outside the home. They were sad and slightly worried by his departure. During dinner, the seats at the head table switched between courses; different groups kept drawing up chairs at Bruggink's table. Nico kept apart and looked on. The psychiatrists sung a song, the managers gave speeches, finally Hein himself spoke: jovial, friendly, controlled. Formerly he had always told the same joke at the conclusion of seminars. They asked for it, every year, and told new colleagues that there would be something special. Nico had been irritated when Hein went from table to table to perform his complicated and rather corny joke everywhere. They were children who had to be humored, always with the same, predictable story. How could Hein accept it and even glory in it and enjoy it? Disgusting.

There was the familiar buzzing once again: The joke! For the last time, the joke!

He went to the toilet. There he encountered Bruggink who

was somewhat furtively tearing paper napkins into pieces at the sink. Questioning, Nico raised his eyebrows.

"You have to let them have their way in small things and go your own way in large matters," said Hein. He tapped his pockets and left.

When Nico came back into the room he saw everyone standing around Bruggink's table in a large circle; there hung a tense silence from which Hein's voice suddenly sounded. The people around him seemed moved, touched; he saw a few women rubbing their eyes, a man balled his fists at his side.

Nico stood watching from a great distance. He understood nothing, but he saw Hein's mouth moving and saw the audience laugh from time to time and then adopt their listening pose once again. It took an eternity. Bruggink coughed affectedly behind his hand. The listeners nudged one another, the last rows raised themselves to their toes. In a final spasm Bruggink spat out a cloud of small, white snippets that landed like snow on the tablecloth.

People shrieked with laughter. Some cried. Bruggink stood up and walked out of the room past Nico.

"You knew it already, didn't you? Remember it well, it'll be up to you next year."

Never, he thought. That's going to change too. I want adult, rational employees, not children you have to lie to and keep quiet with stories. Everyone has to know what is expected, I too. For a minute he saw in front of him a narrow bed, felt the edge of the bed press into his legs; he tucked the blankets in around the child's body, heard himself say reassuring words: Everything's fine, sleep well, tomorrow everything will be the same as today, and it will continue like that always.

Abruptly he turned around to the bar and ordered a whiskey.

Chapter three

Saturday and Sunday were the hardest days. Because the safe network of the school schedule was lacking, she had to force herself to fill the days with activities that held her complete attention. How nice it would have been had she liked sports. Work out, calisthenics, tennis with someone like Aleid Bruggink, with those compact thighs and that square hairdo; take long, ever longer bicycle rides like Nico; think about stomach muscles, position of the back and shoulders, angles between lower and upper leg. She didn't care at all about it, had always hated it and didn't think she could change. The only thing she liked to do was to walk, but in doing that you started to think in spite of yourself, and that wasn't her intention.

The garden. Spring was in the air. She had to engage in a battle against the salty, sandy soil. The vegetable garden became her arena; the sand the enemy, the shovel her sword.

Nico had sneaked away while she was still asleep. Usually he bicycled quickly to the hospital on Saturday, in jeans and a windbreaker. How long can we keep this up, she thought, sitting on the edge of the bed. She bent forward until her head hung between her knees. Every day again try not to think. Disregard with all your might the mute choir in the back of your head that sang "help" at the top of its voice, that chanted incessantly "I wish I were dead." Vigorously limit the unfilled hours of the day by working, answering the mail, taking care of the things in the house, pruning the bushes. And all that silently, separate from each other, alone. He pedaled the hours away on his racing bike; she shoveled them into the ground.

There was still dew on the grass. In the back of the garden, near the gate next to the bicycle path that led to the dunes, the sun was drying the pathetic plants and bushes; a barely visible mist hung above the leaves. Laying out a vegetable garden was a project that would keep her safe for weeks.

Slowly she walked to the shed to get gloves, hoe and spade. She wanted to dig out all the half-dead plants, and next to the shed she made a trash heap of them, a bonfire. Around a plant she pushed open the earth with the spade; sitting on her knees she dislodged the roots until she could pull it out. With a handkerchief she tied back the hair, which kept falling in her face. The muscles in her back were tensed to the limit and hurt. Persevere, she did it for this; for a moment nothing existed outside this struggle.

"Difficult, isn't it, to make something grow in that sand!"

She looked up; she hadn't heard him come, but in her immediate memory she knew that the shells of the bicycle path had crunched. A young man sat on his bicycle; with one hand he held onto the gate and with a foot he balanced on the ground. On the seat rack he carried a large bag of garden soil, and on the handlebars hung plastic bags with the logo of the garden center on them.

"I'm Wessel ten Cate. I attended your school. But only for a very short time. That's how I know you."

Around twenty or so, she thought, a clean-cut face, eyes looking away. Would such a boy be shy? But why then does he speak to me? I can't remember ever seeing him, but that means nothing, students remember teachers better than the other way round. She rose to her feet. Together they surveyed the damage. She told him what she was planning: leeks, lettuce, broad beans, gooseberry bushes, a strawberry bed.

"I can help you if you'd like," he said. "But only on weekends. There is a whole lot of digging."

After all, I really wanted a gardener, she thought. You see, most problems solve themselves. I wish for a young man to do the digging, and here he is. She smiled. His face suddenly broke into a smile. He placed his bicycle against the gate and jumped over it; with both feet he landed in the pile of sand. He extended his hand, she said her name.

"Are you Maj's mother?" he asked.

She nodded, turned around and walked ahead of him to the shed, speaking rapidly over her shoulder. That he should put on an overall which hung in the back on a nail; where the buckets were, the connection for the garden hose, the pruning shears, rope, cow manure, grass seed, flower pots; of course he wanted something to drink—digging makes you thirsty—especially in such beautiful weather; the sun was already hot in that part of the garden…

"Shouldn't we first draw up a plan?" he asked. "I need to know that I'm doing it the way you want."

"Of course," she said, abruptly interrupting her rush, "what a good idea! We'll draw everything in detail."

He sat on the terrace at her garden table with a writing pad in front of him. When she set down the coffee he had already drawn up a plan.

"You have to know about every plant; how deep its roots go and what kind of soil it needs. It's all going to be artificial because there's not much that grows in sand."

"Wessel," she said. "It's Wessel, isn't it? Do you know Maj well? Have you seen her recently? I'm asking you because we haven't had any contact with her for a while and we're worried. Do you know where she is?"

With his pencil he shaded the section of garden where the pines stood and spoke without looking at her.

"At school I sometimes hung around with her. She was special.

I saw her later too, in the city or someplace. But the last time? I'm not so good at dates."

"Maybe you can tell me if you meet her some time?"

The boy nodded; he accentuated the gates around the garden in a dark color and started shading in the driveway.

Later she looked at his back, bent over the shovel. He had left the overalls hanging on the nail and had taken off his T-shirt. His sweat glistened in the sun.

He had asked where he should put the sand that he was taking in full wheelbarrows from the garden. Just run it inside, she had wanted to say. In a flash she had seen the house, crammed with blond grains, choked by immense mountains of sand that came from her garden, making the walls bulge out by the enormous pressure, so that there was no more room, not for her, not for Nico, not for anything from before or now. An inner burial, a sandy stupor, a dusty dying.

"How about the pine forest? Just throw it down there, nothing grows there anyway."

When he said goodbye, a wall of sand had been thrown up between the pine trees, and the vegetable garden looked like an open grave.

"Till next week!" said the young man. He jumped on his bicycle and rode away.

Money, she thought, I should have given him money. Next time mention it right away. Always embarrassing, money.

She felt relieved, actually had become lighter. There was someone who helped her. Not only the extra sand had disappeared, but also the gray hopelessness with which she had woken up that morning. Wessel, she thought, I have Wessel.

She selected translation test passages for the class taking exit examinations, she received parents on parent-teacher evening and met with colleagues about the weak students. A busy week during which she hardly saw Nico. On Friday afternoon she sat with a glass on the terrace, looking at the torn-up garden. The smoke of secrets seemed to spiral up from the holes; she had told no one about her miraculous gardener, not even Nico.

She went inside for a minute to refill her glass. When she came back into the garden, she saw a bicyclist approach, a young man with bicycle shorts and a cap backwards on his head. Her heartbeat quickened—Wessel? With information about Maj? The bicyclist turned into the driveway. It was Nico. He raised his hand, she saw the weird glove with the cut-off fingers, he smiled, and she did her best to wipe the disappointment from her face.

The shiny fabric of the pants accentuated the bulge of his penis. He was wearing an orange shirt with pockets in the back. It was too tight.

For a moment she didn't know what to do; she took refuge in everyday habits and poured him a drink. You fantasize about a young man, he arrives, rushes toward you, and it's a man with lines in his face and bald triangular recesses in his hairline. The cap lay on the table.

"I feel great; it's awfully busy, but I've got plenty of energy. Now that Hein is gone everything is running smoothly, without resistance, without wrangling. I feel like—I feel like it again... it's as if I'm twenty-five again. No, I don't need to eat anything, just give me a glass of water."

She saw that he held in his stomach. He looked at the havoc in the garden, but it didn't seem to get through to him.

Later—he had taken a shower and was wearing regular clothes again—they were sitting in the kitchen at the table.

"Everything is 'care' nowadays, intensive home care, psychiatric care, individualized care. We have care managers and a care office. I'd like to change that; I'm really against it. People shouldn't be taken care of, that's what you do with animals. Patients have to work at their cure, in clear steps, with attainable goals and personal responsibility. That masked use of language is dangerous. Care! Worthless!"

"What if they can't do it or don't want to anymore? After all there are people who can't live by themselves. Do you let them drop dead?"

It was as if he didn't hear her. Perhaps she hadn't even said anything. Did a person have the right not to want anymore at all? Or did you still have to do something? Lie down on rails or jump from a building? She imagined a situation of total indifference, the inability to look ahead, to start moving, to wish for something. Her feet would slip on the slick floor, her back would collapse, she would slowly seep out on the ground while she blew her longings away definitively with her breath. She sat straight up involuntarily and pushed her knees together. Listen. What is he saying? His plate was still filled with potatoes and steak, his wine glass untouched, and he continued talking.

"This afternoon I spoke to the nursing staff to explain my policy. A change in attitude, that's what I demand from them. No more interfering and prohibiting, but figure out how to go on together with the patient. That it *should* go on. Call patients to account about their own part, their task in it. Let them make choices, teach them to look ahead, make them responsible. It caused some commotion, but the atmosphere is good."

She had finished eating long ago and was waiting for an opportunity to talk about the garden and the gardener, but before she was able to get a word in he had already left the table to go and sit at his computer for a bit.

"I've found a gardener," she said to his back.

The kitchen door slammed closed.

The next day it drizzled. Suddenly he was standing by the door in his yellow raincoat. Her joy surprised her. What was so appealing about tramping around a dirty garden on a wet, cold afternoon? Why was it pleasant to be having a conversation with a young man who was a total stranger? She swung the door open.

"Did you feel like coming in this weather?"

He took off his hood and said that this was ideal garden weather, you didn't sweat, saw everything in the right light and avoided dust being blown up. He said it with a crooked, careful smile.

They worked all afternoon, wearing boots. She felt the rain on her cold cheeks and cherished the obsession with which she imposed her will on the garden despite all its resistance. Don't bend, don't give up, and don't lie down.

They sat across from each other in the kitchen, with the light on because it was so gray outside. He had soil on his face, sand in his hair, mud on his hands. Should she offer him the bathroom, or was that going too far? Money, he should have money. Was one hundred Guilders too little?

"I would like to give you money."

He was startled and suddenly put down his mug of tea.

"For Maj?"

What did he mean? Had he misunderstood. Or—would he? She felt herself becoming pale and gripped the edge of the table firmly. Eight white knuckles in a row. Pathetic.

"Do you mean that you've seen her?"

It sounded pretty business-like. It was as if she saw herself, from above, sitting with the young man. Two dark circles facing each other above the light wood of the tabletop. The lamp in between.

"I'm not supposed to tell," he said, hesitating. "She doesn't want it. It's awful; I don't know what to do. But she needs money. I could give it to her and not say where I got it."

Where had he seen her, how did she look, what was she wearing, who was she with, what did she do, what did she say about her and Nico, how did she sound, how did she walk, how? She hung her head and asked nothing.

"Actually I meant that I want to pay you for the work in the garden. Last week I forgot."

"Oh, that doesn't matter," he said with relief in his voice.

She got up and looked for her purse. There, next to the telephone. How can I ever find anything in such a sackful of junk? Wallet. Yes. She pulled out two one-hundred guilder bills which she gave him.

"For now and for last time. Is that OK?"

He nodded, folded up the bills and stuffed them into his back pocket. He stood up, too, and grabbed the dirty raincoat. Strange that a young man like that was so tall. She had to lift her head to look at him.

"I definitely have to go now," he said. "I think it's really unfortunate with Maj. I don't want to do something behind her back that she doesn't want, but I also don't want to lie to you. You have to understand, ma'am, that I can't say anything, not to her and not to you. Otherwise it won't work."

His hand lay on the door handle. He looked past her.

"Won't you please just call me Louise? It feels strange when you're so formal. My students also call me by my first name. I'm used to it."

He nodded. She was out of her mind. What did she want from the boy? It seemed of the greatest importance that he stayed inside, that he would at any rate come back, set a date, not leave her in the lurch. That he smile at her. She was crazy.

"Please sit down for a moment. I have to get something."

Reluctantly he took a step toward the table. She rushed into the living room and started rummaging in a drawer of the cupboard, speaking excitedly over her shoulder in the direction of the kitchen. That she was considering Swiss chard, that she was so happy that something was finally happening in the garden, that without his involvement it would have taken months. Nonsense, all that meaningless chatter. She grabbed all the money she had in the house and put it in an envelope. How lucky that she'd gone by the bank yesterday. Two thousand guilders.

"Here," she said, and held the envelope out to him. "Give this to her. Please."

Hesitating, he took the money and put it in an inside pocket.

"Ma'am you shouldn't, I mean: Louise, you shouldn't be so tense. It'll all work out, it has to."

He placed his hand against her upper arm. It disconcerted her, feeling his strong fingers on her trembling muscles. Now he has to go, she thought, otherwise I'll start to cry.

"I'll call the nursery, I'll order the soil."

She nodded and raised her hand when he disappeared through the dark garden.

Chapter four

The employee-management council was meeting in the old classroom behind the main building. Nico ran over to it, his hair still wet from the shower. Right after his installation as director he had a bathroom constructed in the former filing-room next to Bruggink's old study so that he could ride to work on his bicycle, in a cycling outfit, could pedal himself into a sweat and still be able to appear fresh for the morning report. In the hall between the bathroom and the study there was space for a wardrobe that he had energetically filled with shirts, underpants, socks, a sweater, trousers and jackets. The suitcase had been full; it seemed as if he were moving and was quite satisfied about that. It gave him a pleasant feeling of power to organize the functions of the rooms according to his will. It would never have occurred to Bruggink to undress and bathe at work, but from the beginning Nico had pointed out that he should be able to wash himself if they wanted to have him as director. He would have preferred to get his secretary to do his laundry and iron his shirts.

Without knocking he hurried into the conference room. Jaap Molkenboer, the chairman, was standing next to the blackboard and he used chalk to write down the items on the agenda. *Crisis Center*, Nico saw at a glance, *Forced Job Changes*, *Reorganization* with a big question mark next to it, *Shared Decision-Making!* with an exclamation mark. Sighing, he sank down on a chair at the head of the table. It would last two hours. *Two hours*. He placed his papers in front of him on the table. Without looking around, he knew who was sitting around him because people felt strongly about fixed positions. He felt discontent and negativity hang above the table like smoke. He brought renewal and they were against it.

Right after assuming office as director he had taken an afternoon to explain his plans. His enthusiasm had become stuck in their grumpy-gloomy fault-finding. With dour faces they had listened; I'm not going to fix up the crisis center again, he had said, and all of them had made a note on their notepads at the same time. I'm going to abolish the Therapeutic Community within a limited period. Scratch. Scratch. Admission department number two will be renovated and expanded. A new rehabilitation center will be set up there. Bowed heads. I'm going to terminate the contract for meal delivery to surrounding institutions. New page. There will be a new institutional philosophy, we'll shift the objectives of patient stay and assistance to re-education and the furtherance of independence: I expect the staff members to help us think about it, to take the initiative and be prepared to take refresher courses. At the organizational level what I'm striving for is cooperation with sheltered workshops, with protected living and, at a later phase, with the housing associations in the city.

"That's a reorganization," Molkenboer had said, "for that you need our approval. You can't just change around the whole hospital—that has consequences for the employees and we have to keep an eye on those interests. No, that can't be done just like that. At any rate, I want it in black and white so that we can discuss it in a meeting."

What a pest, he had thought. Molkenboer doesn't feel that he's alive until he obstructs, says no, blocks something. Nico had replied that he'd present a memorandum as soon as possible and that the next work session would be completely devoted to the planned changes.

The chairman had looked at him with a sour little smile. That wasn't possible either just like that; in the employee-management council everything would first have to be discussed, commented on, and examined for possible consequences for the staff. Authorization took a minimum of six weeks; they were swamped but insisted on going through the procedures by the book. It surprised Molkenboer that Nico even considered putting the plan to the organization before the path through the employee-management council had been completed.

Nico had controlled himself. He had written the memorandum during the weekend that followed the meeting; he had thrown the words onto the keyboard rapidly and tensely with hard fingers. Now the document lay on the table.

After two hours it still lay there. They hadn't made any progress. Nico had given his views for the umpteenth time, had discussed the background, had expressed his hope for cooperation, but as he was speaking he heard how impatience crept into his voice. Before it came to an open quarrel, he concluded the meeting. He walked out, treading heavily, Jaap Molkenboer in his wake.

"You're moving so fast, Nico. What's the matter with you?"

"You know exactly what the matter is," Nico said, stiffly. "I've explained it clearly, in terms that can be understood by anyone with an IQ of 90. With examples. Do you want slides?"

"I'm just asking you as a colleague. Why have you become so fanatical, setting yourself against psychotherapy? What's the use of abolishing the Therapeutic Community? Why do you only want to negotiate with patients?"

Nico stopped.

"Because it's the only way to take them seriously. To negotiate is to treat. That's improvement. That's how people get better. Delving into a difficult youth cuts them down. They should be growing instead, from one negotiating position to the next. That way everyone knows what to expect. It's terribly authoritarian to decide for patients. We're going to teach them to make their own decisions."

Molkenboer looked glum. Reluctantly he shifted his enormous fleshy legs in the corduroy trousers and stepped back.

"It sounds good, but still there's something wrong. You're wasting a worthwhile part of psychiatry, and I don't understand why. At any rate, you're going way too fast, and that only arouses resistance. If you go on like that we may make a decision that you won't like."

Nico felt the anger rage through his chest and made a supreme effort to control himself. "Do think about it," he said tersely.

In the parking lot next to a gorgeous car, the personnel manager was chatting with the garage owner. They fell silent when Nico approached.

"For you," said the car dealer. Nico raised his eyebrows.

"I don't need a new one, the one I have suits me very well."

"This is one from the series for directors," said the personnel manager. "Bruggink had one like that too; this is the new model. You have the right to it."

"I don't want it," Nico said impatiently. "It's a pity to waste the money. Meaningless status, conventions, show. Spend the money on something else."

"She drives like a dream, you should try it some time," the garage owner said cheerfully. "It has all the bells and whistles: RVS, PPV, PBS, cruise control, a navigation system, everything!"

Over the man's shoulder he saw Eva walking. In her hand she carried a folded handkerchief with something hanging in it. He said goodbye and followed her.

"Hello." He fell in step with her and looked questioningly at the handkerchief.

"Morels," she said, "just look." She let the handkerchief fall open and showed a small pile of brownish mushrooms with brittle stems. An intense woody smell rose from it.

"You have to let them dry—that makes the poison evaporate and then you can keep them." She refolded the handkerchief. "There is a stand with dozens of them, over there, near those pines. I couldn't resist taking a few with me." She turned around and looked at the row of trees near the exit. The two men were still standing next to the shiny car.

"Do you want to come," said Nico suddenly, "do you want to come and take a test drive?"

They walked back and pulled open the heavy doors.

"I've changed my mind, I'd like to try it after all," he said.

Eva placed the mushrooms on the floor. The car smelled immediately of the woods. He sank down into the soft leather seat that enveloped him. The motor hummed. Gently he let out the clutch. The pebbles crunched, the trees moved alongside, after a couple of supple movements of the wrist the hospital lay behind them and they floated over the road. Eva turned on the radio; he heard a Schubert string quartet with a plaintive, compelling violin melody. She started pushing knobs under the small screen next to the steering wheel. Pinkish oval nails. The road they were driving on appeared on the screen. Like a star the car glided across the sky blue background.

"I've set it for Antwerp," she said. "I'd really like to go there. One hundred and eighty-two kilometers."

I'll take it, he thought. A car with potential; I shouldn't act so timidly; I should enjoy dove-gray leather, music, this motor. He let the car roar for a moment and took the next bend. With open windows he zoomed back into the gates.

On the day of his meeting with Albert it rained. An informal evaluation, Albert had said. The Board of Trustees wanted to keep close tabs during a transition situation; it was Nico's sounding board and support and it valued an open dialogue with the new director. Let's just have dinner together behind the station, Albert had said on the telephone; it's a dump, but the food is excellent and it's a quiet place—they have no music.

The restaurant was on a pier and was surrounded by water on three sides—like a temporarily moored boat, ready to depart again.

He found a parking place for his new car, and with some reluctance left its fragrant warmth to step into the rain. He hadn't taken along a coat; shivering, he hurriedly ran up the pier along the water. Albert came walking up from the other side with a raised umbrella. They shook hands on the planking. Rain hit the black water; waves splashed against the pilings; a yellowish light fell through the restaurant windows.

Albert let him lead the way, across high thresholds, through creaking, narrow doors. A waiter showed them a place in an alcove. The lights of North Amsterdam shone across the wide water.

"I was glad to hear that you accepted the car. You should have suitable transportation; people expect it, and it's good. Do you like how it drives?"

"Perfect," said Nico. "I'm happy with it although I usually go by bike. A no man's land between work and home; you have time to think, you're alone for a moment."

Albert looked at him searchingly.

"You've lost weight. Are you working too hard? Let's agree that this conversation will remain confidential and informal; I just want to get an impression of how you're functioning, if things are to your liking, your view on the course of change, your potential problems in working with some people. Personally, I'd really like to know. The official evaluation will take place later, in a regular meeting. I feel that I've stuck out my neck in appointing you; that's why I'd like to be informed about your progress. A drink?"

While Albert spoke, Nico felt the tension flow from his shoulders. Albert had a dependable haircut: short, a neat parting, small straight hairs escaping at the crown. An impeccable three-piece suit, a tie with bright yellow dots, a boyish voice. They drank. Nico let himself be cradled by the other man's words: that they'd known each other for such a long time, that he was a concerned and hardworking psychiatrist, that it must have been difficult for him to work under Hein Bruggink, to bend to the discipline of the marketplace. Albert admired the way Nico had tried to strive for the real goals of a hospital within that commercial framework.

We're going to give this guy a chance, Albert had said to his fellow board members when Bruggink announced his retirement. Nico had to understand that the Board of Trustees made no policy and made no decisions about the course the hospital should take, that was the privilege of the Board of Directors; the Board of Trustees was only supposed to make certain that there *was* a policy and that it was shaped in a proper way. He, Albert, had had his doubts about Bruggink's approach—a hospital is not a store, but these years had been good economically and there was internal peace as well. Except for the commotion about the crisis center, of course. Personally, between the two of us, he preferred a policy that emphasized content; this evening, in this pleasant alcove, he had an opinion. Less blurring of departments, more specific care and treatment. That's why he had been squarely behind Nico.

"I support you, my boy, you can count on me. Your Planned Approach was clear. What I worry about is the speed with which you're driving it through the organization. People have to readjust; they were salesmen, and they have to become caregivers once again. And then you plan to close departments, shift staff, change functions—all very logical and sensible, but people don't see that right away. They feel discarded."

The pâté was served. Albert had ordered a very good red wine. In the windows Nico saw the reflection of the small, restless waves. He looked at the serious face across from him.

"Well, patience isn't my strongest suit. Once I see where things should go, I want to put it all into practice right away; the rest is dead weight, a waste of time. I know that people find that difficult. They should take courses. The psychiatrists should go on educational trips, to a project with burned-out schizophrenics in America. And in addition have in-house and in-service conferences, have them write articles themselves, hold lectures, draft plans. I *know* it, but I prefer to skip it. Stupid. I've already got the employee-management council against me."

"Yes. Molkenboer called me. All excited, only concerned with being obstructive and putting on the brakes. We've got to do something about that. You need those people badly."

Nico sighed and thought of Molkenboer's well-filled corduroy thighs. It had to be done.

"I'll let up. Draw up an educational plan. A 'learning organization'—what do you think of that? But that Therapeutic Community has had it; I don't want to wait with that. Those therapists will be the first ones to be retrained."

"What do you have against it? These people don't do any harm, do they?"

The main course arrived. With pointed, sharp knives they cut into the dark meat. A second bottle. Across the water a ship sailed, behind its brightly lit windows people stood drinking.

"Oh, they can go their own way, but preferably not on my turf and at my expense. We're here for the real psychiatric disorders, the serious illnesses. They treat problems. That should be done in a problems institute, not in a hospital. It costs lots of money to boot, and the department is never filled. It's a weak spot, in terms of content as well as economics. I don't like vagueness. I want them to make plans, carry them out, and then see if it works. They don't think like that at all."

Albert chewed, reflecting.

"Well, if the occupancy rate is so poor, you should perhaps look at it critically. It will cause a stir. And it's a present for the employee-management council—something to really get their teeth into. According to you it will bring in money?"

"Yes indeed. I'll invest it in the new rehabilitation department. Money well spent."

They fantasized about new buildings, about architects and

contractors, until it was time for dessert, which they both declined in favor of coffee and cognac.

"Ineke told me that she spoke with Louise," Albert said unexpectedly. "She thought Louise was rather quiet. What does she think of your promotion?"

"I don't know. OK I think. She mostly stays out of hospital affairs."

"Busy with her job?"

"Yes. As usual. And she's always busy in the garden."

"I hope you don't mind me saying this, but I think that it is rather important in such an onerous position as yours that you have sufficient support on the home front. Someone who thinks with you, who notices when you're working too hard, someone with whom you can do something relaxing. Well, no two marriages resemble each other of course, but in that respect Ineke has always been very helpful to me. For example, she absolutely insists that I take enough vacation. You should do it too! When did you last get away?"

Nico shrugged his shoulders. He saw the house in the dunes in front of him, with the gloomy row of trees, the driveway, the dug-up garden. He imagined Louise in the kitchen, bent over the plan of her vegetable garden, her face hidden by her dark hair.

"There was always something. And we're limited by school vacations. Louise isn't much of a traveler. Actually, we both like to work hard."

He should stop, Nico thought. Is your marriage all right, do you sometimes go away together, do you regularly have a good conversation? What business is that of his? Soon he'll ask how our daughter—no, nonsense, he knows nothing about that. He couldn't imagine that Louise had hinted at anything about that. Their strongest agreement was that they were silent together, that no name was mentioned, no memory dredged up, no allusion was made. No one came between that. The unmentionable had become the essence of their union. He thought. He straightened his back. Spending time like this at the table, eating and drinking, was pleasant up to a certain point. But there always came a moment when insecurity and powerlessness struck. You had to prevent that, you should never let your vigilance relax; you should always be able to get up in order to go and undertake something.

He said goodbye to Albert, who pensively watched him leave.

Rather the discipline of the market than the terror of kindness, he thought when he trudged to his car. He had drunk too much and was annoyed that he couldn't shake the heavy feeling out of his legs. There was also something wrong with his head; he kept getting caught on words and phrases from the conversation, hobbies, Albert had said, they were important—he went sailing with his sons and he himself tinkered with an antique car. The image of a tippy sailboat with three sturdy men on board was one he couldn't get out of his mind. He shuddered at the thought that Albert would invite him on a weekend to dissect the car motor, or whatever you did with those things. What an idiot he was not to appreciate the friendship of such a nice man. What did he want anyway?

Opposition. Be alert, ready, concentrated. A silent fight, to know who had the power. That the loser would lick his feet made him slightly nauseated. Whoever lost should remain furious; otherwise there was no resistance anywhere. And it was resistance that kept him on his feet. The ferry bumped against the quay and let off a swarm of dark bicyclists who streamed out onto the wet asphalt. The rain had stopped.

He let the motor warm up and basked in the gusts of warm air the fan blew into the car. Slowly he maneuvered his car out of the parking lot. He joined the line of cars that was crawling along behind the station. Under the shield of anger he sensed a desolation that he didn't want; Albert's friendly attitude made him feel lost and caused him to lose his footing. He made him aware that he was inadequate, didn't understand something, didn't feel something. He wasn't able to contemplate the rose. He couldn't do it.

Why was everyone driving so slowly here? The driver of the

car ahead of him had turned his face to the side of the street and seemed to be scanning the back wall of the station. Nico followed his gaze. Women. Whores. Alone, in small groups, leaning against the wall, balancing on the curb. The car ahead of him stopped, a woman with long legs in high, shiny boots bent her tawny face to the door. Nico passed. Slowly.

At the end of the building where the street lighting was dimmer stood two figures. When he came closer, he saw that it was a boy and a girl. The boy leaned with his back against the blank wall and smoked. The girl stood across from him with her arms crossed. Something in her bearing—her skinny shoulders bent slightly forward, her stance with feet placed apart—made him hold his breath. Without his consciously putting on the brakes, the car came to a standstill. He looked.

She wore a gray coat that he didn't recognize, with a hood over her head. Flat shoes—those straight calves!

He made no decision, he had no thoughts, but his right hand opened the window. The boy looked straight at him and, pointing with his thumb, said something to the girl. She turned around. He heard her shoes on the pavement.

The face. The narrow gray eyes somewhat too close together. The wrinkle across her forehead. The expression between fear and contempt. Yes. Yes! He leaned across the passenger's seat and looked sidelong up at her. The mouth was colored dark red; her hair cut short and dyed red. She gave no sign of recognition, only lifted her eyebrows.

"He wants a screw," said the boy. "You can earn something."

She looked over her shoulder and grinned. When she turned back to Nico, the anger burst from her eyes.

"Pervert. Fuck off."

She doesn't see me, he thought. It's not her, I've made a mistake. It's dark in the car; she can't recognize me. He fussed with the light above the rearview mirror, suddenly had the plastic cover in his hands, reached to open the door and in that way get light, he trembled with effort.

"Wait," he said, "wait, I'm coming!"

"Get lost, old man," said the boy, "are you deaf or something?"

The girl bent her head, wreathed with the strange hair, to the window; finally, he thought, she's going to listen.

Suddenly a warm gob of spit hit him in the face, got into his eye, dripped down his chin.

"Pervert," she said once again. She turned around and hand in hand with the young man she walked away.

With icy calm he felt for his handkerchief, wiped his face clean, installed the cover on the light, closed the window, and drove up the road.

Louise was already upstairs; she had turned off the light in the bedroom, but in the kitchen the light over the stove was burning. He took a bottle of beer from the refrigerator and sat down at the table. He drummed with his fingers on the table and waited until the foam in his glass had gone down. No panic. Tomorrow was another day. There should be a plan to restore the relationship with the employee-management council. He had to plan a work session. He would address the employees of the Therapeutic Community. Tomorrow.

He took off his shoes, turned off the light and crept upstairs, like a thief in his own bedroom. Louise was a black spot on the pillow. She had left the curtains open, and his eyes slowly became used to the gray light. Her clothes on a chair. The telephone. The alarm. He tore off his undershirt, flung it on the floor, stepped out of his pants, stripped off his socks. Naked he moved next to her. Sleep, now.

He fell asleep as if he were drowning. Without any protest he sank to the depth where he floated weightlessly while stale air was coming from his nose regularly. With relaxed heaviness his body lay on the mattress.

Reluctantly he drifted to the surface when a shrill ring could no longer be ignored. He pushed himself halfway up, staring in surprise at the alarm clock and the telephone. For a moment he didn't understand what was the matter.

"Telephone," said Louise, "are you awake?"

He took the phone. His voice rasped when he said his name.

"Fire! In Duinrand. Fire department's on its way...You've been notified according to the disaster plan. Are you coming?"

"Of course. I'm coming! I'll be there as soon as possible."

In the half dark he saw Louise's eyes gleam. She was watching him get dressed, her hands lay open on the comforter, white, powerless. Something pushed forward in his thoughts, something from yesterday, something beyond words. Away with it; where are the socks, a sweater, keys?

"I have to leave now. Fire alarm. Maybe it's a drill; if so I'll be back soon."

He rushed down the stairs, grabbed a leather jacket from the coat rack and slammed the door shut behind him. Outside it smelled of salt and damp sea air. Before he got into the car, he looked up at the pale shadow in the window, who waved at him. He waved back.

Childishly excited he raced to the hospital, with his brights on, going far too fast. He whistled a tune, pinched his thighs and chuckled. It was unseemly to look forward to a fire, but it couldn't be helped. He drove with open windows but couldn't smell anything yet. It wasn't until he turned into the hospital grounds that he realized that it was serious: in the back, near the railway, hung deep black, greasy smoke clouds. He parked and started running, first on the wide path, later cutting through by way of narrow trails. Tree branches hit him in the face and a burnt smell invaded his nostrils. In the distance he could hear the fire sirens.

Closer by, voices rang out; hurried commands of the staff, frightened cries of the patients. Strange that you could generally recognize someone as a patient by his voice. Would be a good research project. Voice diagnosis. Please speak. Thank you, now I know.

He slowed his pace. Duinrand Pavilion was being consumed in a crackling fire and was sending out enormous waves of heat. Scorched leaves hung straight down on the trees across from the entrance. A group of patients in pajamas, barefoot, was being taken to a safe distance by Erik with the heavy arms. A fire truck was coming up the wide path; people drew back, shouted, screamed. With a bang a window burst into pieces; dirty yellow flames spewed out. For a moment Nico, fascinated, listened to the sounds. The fire roared, whispered, gnawed, tapping and crackling at the woodwork, whistled, drafted, and sputtered. He shook his head and went toward Erik.

He found him slightly to the side of the entrance, pale but undaunted. He shook Nico's hand—it made a bizarre impression. Perhaps it underlined the seriousness of the situation, thought Nico, but you could also see it as congratulations: a completely obsolete pavilion removed without charge, and insurance money to boot for a beautiful new building. Erik certainly didn't think like that, certainly not now.

"Were you able to get everyone out?"

Erik shrugged his massive shoulders.

"I don't know yet. I believe that we emptied the sleeping quarters, but whether everyone was there? Some people jumped through the windows—Johan, for example, holding Mrs. Van Overeem by the hand! It's chaos. It went so fast. We were drinking tea, and suddenly we smelled it. Door open: flames! That means the smoke detector wasn't working."

"And no sprinklers either, I assume?"

"No, we don't have those. I'm going to take my people to the main cafeteria. Two colleagues from the night shift are still searching, and the trainee girl too. To see if there are still people in the bushes."

"I'm going to look too. See you in a moment!"

Nico started to walk around the burning building, looking in the shrubbery for patients who had fled. Through the broken windows he saw burning beds, lace curtains like flaming flags, curling melting bits of linoleum on the floor. Everything was being destroyed, devastated, and wiped out. He felt his heart leap and was ashamed of it.

The stench was unbearable and he took out his handkerchief

to hold it in front of his nose. Slowly he edged along the shrubbery to the gate and scanned the area carefully, his eyes tearing. At the gate something moved, a dark shape crouched on the ground—an animal, a frightened patient, a wounded nurse? He ran toward it, stumbled, hooked his foot in a blackberry vine and approached, cursing. It was Eva.

She lifted her head from her knees when he said her name. She had flung her arms around her legs; she sat against the gate like a compact lump of misery. Messy hair, a smeared face, a bleeding hand. He kneeled in front of her, spit in his handkerchief and began to wipe her cheeks clean.

"Are you that frightened, what happened to you, do you have pain, can you stand?" He murmured softly to her pale face and didn't expect an answer.

"Come, I'll help you get up, just hold on to me." He pulled her up, slowly, carefully, taking care that she couldn't possibly fall down. He picked a scorched leaf from her hair, stroked her cheek consolingly.

Her lips began to tremble and he felt her shoulders shake. It wanted to get out; the horror fought a way up and out.

"Mr. Van Raai," she bawled. Suddenly there were tears, and her face was wet. Her voice became fuller; the words came rapidly and uncontrolled; between snot and slobber her story came out. She screamed it into the hollow between his arms.

When the fire broke out they had been sitting in the office, by coincidence the night staff had just come. They had run into the sleeping quarters, awakened the patients and made them leave their beds. There was no time to put the people who couldn't walk into wheelchairs; Erik had carried them out on his back one after the other. She had herded the walking patients ahead of her through the hall to the door that was opened by the head of the night shift. Erik screamed that she should go to the small rooms; there were people who slept in the small one- or two-person rooms at the end of the hall. Not all of them were occupied; if it was at all possible people were put in the ward, which was better for social intercourse and easier to oversee for the staff. At night these small rooms were locked from the outside. Otherwise people would wander and prowl around.

She had tried to get closer but the fire raged at the end of the hall; it was impossible to reach the doors. She could no longer find Erik.

She ran outside and saw Johan, the nervous young man, step through a broken window. A heavy woman was standing behind him, and he helped her attentively over the windowsill. She pointed out to them where they should go and kept running to the back of the pavilion. There was Mr. Van Raai's room, brightly lit by the flames. Mr. Van Raai himself was sitting in the middle of the room in his wheelchair, impassive, his hair ablaze. In front of the window, outside, the bushes were burning. There was no way to get through. She had screamed and pointed, but no one could do anything.

"He just burned! I was standing near, I saw it!"

Nico caressed the sooty hair, whispered: "Be still, be still, it's over, there now ..."

"He did nothing! He just sat there! He was burning!"

She sobbed, she sniffed, she sucked in the dirty smoky air.

"And I did nothing!"

"You couldn't do anything. You tried everything. Be still."

He held her tight and placed a hand on her cheek. She looked at him, piercing, distraught.

He put his arms around her body, caressed the narrow back, placed the flat of his hands on her moving flanks, rubbed until she quieted down, moved down and up, a breast, a surprising softness, the angle of a hip, a shoulder that conformed to his hand—suddenly there was a warm woman in his arms whom he clasped against him, whom he wanted to feel from head to foot, wanted to swallow up and press to bits—whom he embraced.

With his hot, cracked lips he blew over her eyebrows, with his excited tongue he licked the tears from her eyes, with his nose unsettled by smoke he sniffed the warmth from her neck. A smell of long ago, a young animal smell, a young girl's smell, a girl's aroma, burnt spring. He felt her hand in his neck, her fingertips along his ear, he smelled her agitated breath. Then he took her face between his hands and he devoured her mouth. She opened her lips so that he could feel her teeth, could taste her saliva, could search for her warm tongue. He didn't think. Leaning against the broken-down chicken wire, he was doing what had to be done, without reservations. This was it. Behind him he heard the hissing of fire hoses, the crackling of fire, the splitting of wood and the cracking of glass. A great destruction was taking place at barely fifteen feet away, but he stood solidly on two legs and caressed a girl, a woman who had come out of the fire to kiss him. This was now.

Chapter five

She sat at the big table and translated Tacitus. Of all the writers she taught, he was her favorite, with his poignant drifting between cynicism and compassion and his sublime balance between form and content. But she didn't lose herself only in the play of words and sentences; she listened with a hungry substratum of her senses to *what* the great historian said, she looked for the reason for the compelling phrasing and sighed with satisfaction when a sharply carved pair of words fit exactly with their meaning. It was about power.

At one time she had been a member of a reading group, a group of six women and two men that met once every two weeks to discuss a book that had been read by all. At one of the first meetings, a collection of stories to be discussed was by a writer who announced on the back flap that he wanted to "disorder the language." First, in sheer admiration, she had marveled at that intention, but later, alone on her way home, she had become raging mad, talking out loud and cursing in her small car. The arrogance of such an author, the megalomaniac folly of such an aim, the lack of insight into what kept people going that was revealed by such a phrase! How did he dare?

And the publisher printed it proudly, as a recommendation for the reader who in his snobbishness probably found it quite interesting. Disorder the language. You couldn't disorder something unless you mastered the rules, unless you stood above them, unless you could oversee the whole at any moment. So that's what he was professing to be, that storywriter.

She had let herself be driven into a corner by the enthusiastic conversation of the reading group members, silent, weighed down by the realization that everyone knew what it was about, except she. The readers knew the rules of the language and found it fascinating when they were broken, when the writer showed how you could remain master of the language.

No one paid attention to the underlying dependence of the language, to the notion that without the tight fabric of words and their mutual connections any thinking was impossible. Nor had she, she'd let herself be intimidated and overawed, and only in her car could she figure out that she had another opinion. That she was happy with the straightjacket of language, grateful for the structure and the limitations; that every day she was conscious of the blessings of the rules. She knew about disordered language from Nico's patients. Alzheimer's devoured the brains of old people so that they could no longer find any words. Tumors and hemorrhages affected the speech center in healthy adults so that from one moment to the next they could say only one little phrase that they had to use for everything! Diabolic schizophrenia made young people experience language in a new way so that words received unsuspected, threatening meanings and so much power that they could kill. No, preferably no disorders.

Why hadn't she been able to say this under the modern designer lamps with the red wine? She wasn't suited for social intercourse, she couldn't think until she was alone. She had withdrawn from the reading club and had flung the book of the disordering writer in the wastebasket.

Now she concentrated on Tacitus and tried diligently to fathom the rules of his language. Every time she seemed to succeed it gave her a feeling of contentment and reassurance. Perhaps you can never understand exactly what someone is thinking, but you can at any rate find out how he says it. If you do your best.

The doorbell. A truck from the garden center had backed into the driveway. In front of her stood the driver's helper, with paper and pencil in hand. Over his shoulder she saw the loading platform rising. The black earth started to shift, on the surface particles and clods of soil began to move and slide down onto the pavement; the largest part of the mass seemed to cling to the edge for a moment but collapsed under its own weight and from the increasingly steeper incline it thudded heavily to the ground.

"Just a quick scrawl right here," said the man who stood on her step. She took the pen, signed, and remained motionless, watching how the truck lowered the platform and disappeared on its large wheels.

Where Nico's car was supposed to stand there was an enormous pile of fertile soil, a dark promise of future growth.

It wasn't until then that she saw the badly mauled lawn. Her pride and joy had been damaged by a diligent or desperate mole, which during the night had raised numerous molehills all over the exposed surface of the small lawn. Molehills of sand.

However you covered it, pushed it aside and buried it, the hated element found a way up. The small lawn winked at her with malicious pleasure and carefree superiority. She slammed the door closed. With shovels she would spread new soil over the garden, she would dig away the sand piles, cover the grass with soil, fill the holes. She would call Wessel, she wouldn't give up, and she would stand up to Nico's irritation about the obstructed driveway.

Instead, she dragged her bicycle out of the shed and rode to the city, not over the bicycle path through the dunes, but straight across the polder that reassured her with its regular rectangles and straight ditches, as though no violence had been used here. She knew that she lied to herself. Landscape was war, just like the hospital, the school, and the family. The polder was a living reproach to the water, enslaved and exploited land that was intent on revenge. Having to adjust yourself to the dikes, letting your usefulness be measured in terms of grass production, always being thirsty. Did she experience it like that? Louise thought. Was our child a still, dried-out pasture, drained soil, too exhausted to fulfill expectations? Were we the ones who serviced the pumping engine, drained away the water, established the allotment?

Nico, she thought, Nico who couldn't stand any weakness or powerlessness. And I who went along with it, she thought, pedaling doggedly, squeezing her hands tightly around the handlebars. Too cowardly to say no, too unsure to go against his certainties, too afraid to make him angry. But he was already angry. Angry because the long-awaited child remained quiet and fearful, didn't seem to have any fun, and performed poorly in school. She should have insisted on having Nico arrange for the child be seen by a colleague of the poetic professor; someone should really have looked at her, become aware of her nature and her condition, however difficult or terrible. But she hadn't done that, out of fear that Nico's anger would shift to her. In this way she, too, had become an extortionist, an oppressor, someone who makes demands. An accomplice.

Structure, Nico had said, and clear tasks. It's quite possible that the starting point isn't too favorable, but a person doesn't only consist of genetic material. Environmental influences are at least as important. We have to make demands on her, encourage her to stimulate her development, ignore negative behavior. If you pay attention to complaining, crying, and refusing, then you only encourage these things.

The child didn't let herself be stimulated to make headway. It seemed as if the demands were too heavy and didn't challenge her to action. What Nico called negative behavior wasn't really there. She didn't say no, she cried very little and wasn't difficult. She was gray. And quiet.

The pastures gave way to gardens and houses. Without noticing, Louise had slowed down and glided slowly past the flowerbeds.

The soil must be very fertile here; daffodils were blooming in brilliant yellow, bushes and shrubs displayed swollen buds, the grass was sturdy and lush. A man with pruning shears in his hands stood near a low hedge. Behind him was a low, wide house with a thatched roof. Something familiar in his bearing made her brake, and she stood still for a moment, balancing herself with one foot on the curb. The man she saw, his back in a moss-green windbreaker, stood up straight in the middle of his domain and lifted the shears.

He had pruned the apple trees in front of the house to the bone and now he was busy cutting the hedge back to hip level. Cutting back and cutting short was the only thing that Nico did in the garden from time to time; he would carry on doggedly and purposefully against the vegetation but wanted nothing to do with planting, tying up and looking after. Males like to prune, she thought, while she was watching the hedge shoots falling down. Males are afraid that they themselves will be snipped and clipped; they want to be one step ahead of the enemy and go on the attack. Pruning is a defense against the fear of the cleaver. She smiled. The man turned around, as if he felt her eyes on his back, and looked at her. He greeted her, a friendly smile appearing on his face. He placed the hedge-clippers at his feet and came toward her. Reaching over the disfigured hedge, he shook her hand. Albert, Albert Tordoir. Nico's supervisor, Ineke's husband.

"Louise! What a coincidence to see you. I wanted to call you." His face darkened. Suddenly she saw how he would look in court: stern, fair, ordinary. There was something piercing and searching in his glance, and she looked away to the garden. He had roses. He could. There was no sand here; the soil was substantial and generous.

"Come in for a moment, I'll make you a cup of coffee."

She rolled her bicycle into the garden and leaned it against the garage. Welcoming, he held the kitchen door open for her.

The kitchen was less modern and flashy than she had expected. Lots of woodwork and open cupboards with cluttered dishes in them. Nice, actually. Would his wife still be in bed?

"Ineke is playing tennis. She told me that she spoke with you recently."

She remembered the perfectly dressed woman on the terrace. How could he be married to such a woman? Perhaps she saw it wrong and Ineke was nicer, or different, than she thought. He has a friendly face. He actually *was* a calm and pleasant person; she had sat next to him during special hospital dinners and had felt at ease with him.

"The other day I had dinner with Nico. You probably know that. That's the reason I wanted to call you. I hesitated. And now you're in my kitchen!"

It started to smell of coffee. He filled two mugs and sat down across from her.

"To tell you the truth, I'm worried about Nico, and I'd like to know if you share these worries. Sugar?"

She shook her head. What does he mean, what does he *know*? She thought of the text she had read that morning—full of plotting, machinations, insinuations in boudoirs and brothels. How the courtiers tried to get into the good graces of the rulers and then resorted to conspiracies. The hidden meaning in everything that happened.

Did he want to conspire with her against Nico? She had to remain watchful and not yield to friendliness. But how gladly she would drop all defenses; she felt it in the tension of her muscles. Let it go, give in, tell him everything.

Meanwhile Albert continued talking.

"We are very happy with him, we're enormously appreciative that he is taking on the challenge by himself. Of course we already knew him as a rather active and decisive psychiatrist. He has ideas, and we were glad to place him in the position where he can carry them out."

Yes, appreciation, that was good, she thought. They should be happy that Nico took on the whole organization himself, gave direction to policies, and didn't avoid difficult decisions.

"But I'm worried."

Albert stirred his coffee and didn't look at her.

"I would like this to go well. A new direction that should have a chance of succeeding. We think, I think, that Nico is the right man in the right place, at the right time as well. *But…*"

Why was she actually sitting here? What did he want to get off his chest? Why was she going to listen to it? What did she herself think of it? When could she leave?

Nico was proceeding very brashly, she heard Albert say. And because of that he was rubbing many people the wrong way—the employee-management council for example. These last weeks Nico appeared to have little patience; it seemed as if he had difficulty realizing what effect his plans and measures might have on others. Formerly, he used to show more understanding.

"So I thought: is there something wrong? I shouldn't ask you, I know that. But I'm doing it anyway. Are there problems? Between you? With your daughter? Sorry."

It's none of his business, she thought, that's what I should say. He has nothing to do with it; he has no right to ask me such questions. I don't have to answer. Or will I put Nico in danger then? Perhaps he's right, perhaps Nico is slipping and something is totally wrong. I'm no use to him, I never say anything, I don't dare to take up a position. I live only partially. Since she's been gone. Even before that.

"Say something," said Albert. "Did I frighten you? I'm asking it as a friend, I'm worried and perhaps you are too. He came down very hard on Jaap Molkenboer; it's not like the Nico I know. And when I went out for dinner with him recently I found him quite frankly preoccupied. Worse than absent-minded."

Like the ocean at retreating tide it tugged at her: she should understand, support, help him. That's what a wife did for a husband, that's how it should be.

To her surprise she got up. It felt completely natural, she stood calmly behind her chair and took her purse from the back.

"You're right," she said to the man across from her, "you're not in a position to ask me these questions, and I wouldn't be able to answer them. The hospital is your problem, your life. I don't want to be involved in that."

She was silent for a moment.

"I'm jealous of your roses, they look so healthy."

She was halfway outside when he rose to his feet and followed her. His face looked closed and upset. She continued talking and heard that her voice sounded lower than usual. Before she knew it, she had shaken his hand and was back on her bicycle.

Nico was heatedly talking into the telephone when she came home. His trousers hung in folds over his buttocks and his shirt was too loose around his neck.

With a short, barking acknowledgment he slammed the receiver down.

"Damn it! Now the management is also being obstructive! General and Technical Services at any rate, they want to continue making money from their superb kitchen. And Research Services which has a project running in a department that I'm going to close."

He bounced back and forth from heel to toe. The fighting stance.

She was silent.

"And the head of training has objections to abolishing the Therapeutic Community. He said it's the only department where his residents can still learn something about psychotherapy. That's exactly why I want to get rid of it, it leads to nothing! They've been scheming together behind my back; during this morning's meeting not a cross word was spoken. And then these phone calls to me at home! What do you think of that?"

She picked up the newspaper. Slowly she raised her head and looked at him. His grim face, his compressed lips.

"If those ideas of yours are so good, why is everyone against them?"

He was startled. She could tell from the sudden stiffening of his shoulders.

"Are you abandoning me too? How can you say that? You don't know anything about it."

"I'm not saying anything," she said calmly. "I'm not abandoning you. I'm only asking a question. Nothing else."

She unfolded the paper. The letters of the black headlines

danced in front of her eyes. For the second time that day a speechless man was standing across from her. He had counted on yielding sand, but crashed to bits against a dam of basalt. Look at him standing there, she thought. Lost, irritated because she acted differently from what he was used to. She was aware of her wildly beating heart; the newspaper rustled between her trembling hands. What was happening? As if they were dancing on untrodden ground.

"Explain it to me once more," she said softly.

He remained standing and looked down at her, sighing.

"It's about the illusion of curing. That's why they call the institution a hospital, thus it seems that there exist real diseases that can be treated and cured. Sometimes that's so, but most of the time it isn't; if you're after curing, you'll be disappointed time after time and in the end you become embittered and unsure. That whole empathizing and understanding crowd starts from the premise that you can get them back in shape. You let them see the chart, you explain what can be seen—historically, genetically, dynamically—with pain and difficulty you make changes and then the cure is achieved. A fable, a pipe dream, a lie. That therapists' clinic wants to see it like that, and that's how they see it, but it's nonsense. For most of the so-called psychiatric illnesses there exists no cure. You're powerless, you can't do anything. Therefore you shouldn't want to. People should use their reason more. Especially physicians."

"You exaggerate. It can't be that simple. What's wrong with understanding?"

While she was speaking she thought: Don't do it, keep your mouth shut, let him talk. Louise placed her feet next to each other on the floor; she folded her arms in front of her chest and squeezed her lips together.

"Everything!" he roared. "Shall I give you an example? Take infertility, a woman who can't have children. Do you have to understand, empathize, make it clear psychodynamically? That only makes you more miserable, and it cures nothing. What you should do is survey your options and make a step-by-step plan. In vitro fertilization. Implantation of a donor embryo. Fill in adoption papers. Do things.

Action, work. People wallow in their powerlessness but just one change of perspective is sufficient to regain control over your life."

She looked at his hands, his powerfully formed hands with the pronounced knuckles and the raised veins. You recognized the doctor by the short, clean nails. Psychologists often had nails that were too long and dirty. It doesn't touch me, she thought, it's not about me; it's about him. I don't want it to touch me. I'm only looking.

"I would like to close down the hospital," he said. "After my term as director there should only be a first-aid station where psychotic or depressed people can be put on medication. At most for two months. After that, they go to residential and work facilities in the city. Or wherever. The hospital grounds become a park."

His voice sounded flat and controlled. Everything on him had become taut recently: his muscles, his face, his eyes.

A strange shift had taken place in how he looked, in what he said. Everything was correct but it was also nonsense. She thought of dike subsidence, how in broad daylight a sunny, grassy dike could collapse and disappear because the underlying sandy foundation had started to move and was washed away. Unreliable sand.

"It's not that I hate my work or detest the hospital. I want effectiveness. Scrap excessive and meaningless things. These managers can all go; what they're thinking up is no good to anyone. They don't have the feeling that they're working until they're changing and fouling up all sorts of things. No one is waiting for that. You know, I think I'm going to take a quick bike ride."

She saw him turning onto the bicycle path with his bare legs and his youthful cap. She had a pain in her stomach, and a sickly stuffy feeling behind her eyes. She remained sitting on the couch with her hands in her lap while evening fell.

Outside, the great mountain of garden soil was waiting, as motionless as she. Now that the turbulence of Nico's words had drained away, nothing stirred anymore. He had made professional pronouncements and had referred to a scientific medical example. Yet, she had reacted as if she had been beaten up and knocked down. Was that because of disordered language? No, not the language but the relationship between language and what language refers to had been disordered. He meant something, she'd misconstrued it. If she could receive the message in another way, nothing would be the matter. She herself was in charge of that. Except it wasn't true. It was much more complicated. He said something but meant something different, something that perhaps he didn't know himself. She wasn't in charge of anything, she had no power. It was her own fault; *her* language had been detached from the usual rules, she had done it.

She missed him, the man, the youth who had made her a companion of his ambitions. His joy and his fear were gone, perhaps for almost twenty years. She had placed her hand along his cheek, kissed his hard lips before he left for the weekly lecture of the hated professor. She had known what he thought, what he felt. She missed him.

She opened the door of the third room carefully. She didn't turn on the light but moved the yellow curtains aside so that the twilight came in. She stood in the middle of the room and looked around. The cupboard with the children's books. The tall shelves with toys. The small desk with the name scratched in deeply. The closed wardrobe. The narrow bed. Nothing hung on the wall. There was no mess anywhere. She stood with her feet together stiffly and took shallow breaths. She was a guilty tourist in the children's museum.

In the hall, on the stairs, she regained command over muscles and weight. She stomped downstairs and started to arrange her desk with big gestures. She slammed the paperwork for school onto the table; she placed the bank statements and bills in front of her in small stacks. When Nico returned she was irritably filling in payment orders. The time for dinner had passed somehow; she wasn't hungry and he didn't ask for it. Time is place, she thought. If we were sitting in the kitchen it would be dinnertime. But if I'm in her room, children's time is still inaccessible. I mustn't think further, I must keep busy with what presents itself: the bills. Vaguely she heard the clatter of the shower upstairs; somewhat later she registered that he had come down the stairs, walked toward her and remained standing behind her chair.

"Are you managing?"

She turned around on her chair and looked at him.

"No," she said. "I have an enormous bill from the garden center and there's not enough in my account anymore to pay it. Perhaps you could do that?"

He nodded and walked to the window. Was he looking at the mountain of soil? Did he see his own reflection in the black glass?

"How can it be that you have no more money? I'm happy to pay it, but I don't understand it at all. Where has your salary gone?"

Now, she thought, I have to say it now.

"I've given it away."

Incredibly stupid. Such a helpless, naïve remark. Given away. As if she were going through the streets with a jingling moneybag to distribute charity to drifters.

"I paid the gardener," she said. She tried to make her voice sound steady and convincing.

"How much?"

"Twenty-five thousand."

Now he'll get furious. Spitting with rage he'll now call me everything weak and stupid, he'll wash his hands of me.

But he started to roar with laughter. Shrieking he slapped his knees and the tears splashed from his eyes.

"The gardener! The lucky gardener!"

He flopped down on a chair and placed his arms on the table. He let his head rest on them. Hiccupping and gasping his words came out.

"Excellent! I hope that you'll enjoy it a lot. The garden. It costs a tidy penny, but at least you've *got* something."

When he had quieted down he stood up again. He pulled her up and embraced her.

"My Louise. You're so unpredictable. Independent. And such decisions you make. I love you, really."

Under the influence of his explosive cheerfulness she started to smile although she felt far from cheerful; the grimaces on her face seemed to call up pleasure gradually—perhaps she was relieved that she escaped the expected anger, perhaps it did her good to hear him laugh again; she didn't know and she didn't really care. Roaring with laughter they rolled together through the room while he kept shouting "the gardener, the gardener" and she answered "twenty-five thousand guilders."

They clasped each other, desperately, she thought for a moment, no: happy, relieved, hopeful.

At the bottom of the stairs they stopped. He kissed her, with arms around each other's waists they walked up the stairs. Don't look at that door, that closed door, keep on going to the bed, flop down on it still shaking with laughter, feel his weight, receive his body with hers, adjust arms, legs, stomach to that heavy, that ominous and fiery body which took possession of her where she lay.

He slept. The smile had been wiped from his face and had given way to a grim, embittered expression. He lay flat on his back, his head in the middle of the pillow, the hands balled into fists on his chest. She pushed her hand under them and curled up at his side. She brought her head next to his and almost touched his ear with her lips.

"It's not true," she whispered. "It wasn't for the gardener. Why should I give that boy so much money? That wouldn't make any sense. He's not just a garden helper, he's a messenger. He helps me. He knows Maj."

She waited a moment, but he didn't react. His breath continued to flow evenly, nothing changed in his position, his eyelids lay smooth above the cheeks.

"He took the money for her. To buy a place to live, to purchase things, to live. He never says anything about it, I don't ask, I give the envelope and he nods and puts it away. I give the money to my daughter, our daughter. Like any mother. That's how it is."

Nico snored. Suddenly he turned toward her and flung an arm around her.

"The gardener," he slurred, "you're talking about the gardener!"

He chuckled and pressed her closer to him.

"Yes," she said. "Yes."

Chapter six

He pressed the button of the bike computer when he wheeled into the gate. Five seconds slower than yesterday. Shit. His calves felt as if they were filled with mush and he was out of breath. His new silver car stood shining quietly in the parking lot. Was he out of his mind to be killing himself on his bike? Any other person wouldn't let himself be deprived of the pleasure of driving such a splendid car. His T-shirt was soaked and he felt a dull pain in his back. Persevere, don't give up. The body should adjust; he shouldn't give in but make demands calmly and decisively, every day over again. With his hand on the narrow saddle he steered the bicycle inside, past the porter's lodge where a man with thick glasses and an open mouth was staring at a screen.

"Good morning!"

The man turned his face to Nico and got ready to say something. Nico didn't wait for it and let the self-closing glass door fall closed behind him. He placed his bicycle in the unused dishwashing kitchen at one end of the hall and marched to his room. The door stood open. Strange. Perhaps Alice was tidying his desk. She shouldn't do that. Take a nice shower in a moment, after that he'd feel better. He heard a buzzing as he came closer. Was a cleaning crew still at work? Cigarette smoke drifted toward him, it made him furious, he didn't want any smoking in the main building, and he had made that clearly known. He took a deep breath to vent his wrath forcefully and stepped into his room.

The words stuck in his mouth from surprise. The room was filled with people, at least twenty-five according to his quick estimate. They leaned against bookcases, sat on the desk, in the windowsills, on the floor. They smoked cigarettes they had rolled themselves and chewed gum. Young people, some with aggrieved expressions on their faces, others reckless, but all were tense and disgruntled.

The talking had ceased but no one looked at him. A young man with an enormous body sat on the exercise bike with his head bent over the dial.

Nico remained silently standing in the doorway, painfully aware of his bare legs and the small cap on his head. Eventually a woman of about thirty slid off the desk. She shook her loose hair, clasped her hands behind her back, and with her chin raised she began to speak.

"This is a sit-in."

It came out somewhat hoarsely. She cleared her throat and started again.

"We have taken over your room. We're not leaving until our demands are met. We want the Therapeutic Community to continue. It's absolutely essential. We have to remain there. It's time to bring this abuse of power and scrapping of services to an end. We demand continuity.

"Patient council," whispered a young man on the desk.

"We have informed the patient council; they agree with us. Jos here is part of it. We think this is so serious that we have taken action ourselves. As patients of the Therapeutic Community and of the outpatient clinic."

A young man stuck a paper in her hand.

"This is a letter with our demands. We're presenting it to you. We want to stay. Shutting down is shutting out. Long live the Therapeutic Community!"

There was a half-hearted cheer. The woman handed Nico the letter. He showed no sign of accepting it but continued watching silently. The man on the exercise bike looked at his watch.

"I have to go to therapy," he said. "I'll be back in an hour."

Clumsily bumping into his fellow-occupiers he walked to the door.

Nico looked at the dirty sneakers, the stained pants, the large, swollen face and was aware that an ice-cold rage was rising within him. Look at them sitting there, he thought, too afraid to become angry, filled with resentment but not able to express it in an adult manner. They're children! Yet too big and too unsure to be children. How overconfidently they must have forced their way into his room; they had probably let themselves be put up to it by their cowardly therapists—be assertive, follow your own feelings—who, themselves, were of course sitting tight in their safe treatment rooms awaiting developments. Children in their thirties who were too stupid to see through the strategy of those treating them, who let themselves be exploited with enthusiasm, who sat on his desk with their lazy bottoms and handled his papers with their nervous fingers. Who let their dirty ash fall on his carpet.

The tall youth wanted to leave, but Nico stood in the doorway and didn't budge.

"May I come through? I have to go to therapy."

He could smell the sour odor from the dirty clothes. An acrid undertone: cold sweat. Why didn't he feel sorry for the youth, and a patient to boot; why did he feel himself getting angrier by the minute, having to force himself to hold his hands still against the doorpost? They have to leave, he thought, they should have left long ago. Children have to leave home, run away, plan their own life and not sit around and wait to see if their parents become angry when they disobey. Not sit on the floor and beg to stay, please! They should go, leave the grounds, and get themselves out and into the city!

His hand trembled when he let go of the doorpost. He turned around and stomped out.

The contact with the hard ground did him good. He walked faster and faster, until he reached his familiar running pace. Running steadily and controlled, on his way to the building where the Therapeutic Community was located. Fleeing. His legs had made it clear to him that he had to leave his occupied room. But why? He was a psychiatrist; he knew what to do with a group of anxious, insecure, angry people. Didn't he? He had learned how to act, how he should behave. But he hadn't done it; he'd fled. From the ineffectual dissatisfaction that arose from the group? Of course not. From the firm and clear desire not only to mercilessly curse and humiliate the tall youth who had sat on his exercise bike, but also to actually kick the hell out of him and pull his arms from his body, stomp his fingers to pieces, bash in his eyes. The destruction of the helpless, that's what he was fleeing. He felt that impulse in his muscles; it was in the force with which his feet hit the pavement. The doctor as executioner. A chill, restless wind blew.

Among the waving treetops he saw the yellow painted building where his feet led him. He slowed down, got his breath under control, and reduced his steps.

Jaap Molkenboer stood smoking a pipe in front of the entrance and looked up surprised when Nico approached. He stared at Nico's bare legs, at the narrow sports shoes and at the sweaty shirt. Questioning, he raised his eyebrows.

"Aren't you carrying this health regimen too far?"

"Prick," said Nico. "Coward. Placing a bunch of weaklings in my room and staying out of range yourself. How dare you?!"

The surprised face became smooth and expressionless. The pipe was knocked against the wall to remove the ashes. Tap, tap, tap.

"It was an independent decision of the patient population. They're unanimous about resisting your policy. We do too, you know that, but we have our own channels. Not that we've got anywhere that way, but that's because of you. Simply extending your hand would have been sufficient. If you had said: OK, we're going to confer, we'll set a date. Amicably. As adults. Then none of this would have been necessary. As I told you the other day: you're wrecking the organization, and it puzzles me why you're doing it. You don't seem to be a masochist. Those destructive tendencies are a mystery to me. Too bad that you've never been in analysis."

"What a sanctimonious asshole! You're afraid for your own position and send a little army of the helpless out to defend you. Hypocrite!"

"This is a pointless discussion," Molkenboer said calmly. "You're confused, perhaps you should take some time off. I won't try to conceal it from you that it pains me: first the elimination of the crisis service and now the closing of the Therapeutic Community. There was probably an economic necessity for the first; for the second I can see only personal motives. You begrudge others the psychiatric treatment that couldn't help your own daughter. Sorry, but that's how I see it."

A short movement with enormous force. A muffled cracking, an interrupted cry, a dull thump. Molkenboer lay bleeding on the bricks, his hand in front of his nose.

"Board of Trustees," he whispered, "inform the employee-management council, immediately. Intimidation, mistreatment, mis, mis..."

Pink air bubbles between the fingers. Silence. Nico looked surprised at the bent figure; with his foot he pushed the cracked pipe into the shrubbery. He felt light in the head. At a calm pace he started back, the thin soles of his shoes skimming over the pavement. He felt dizzy. He should sit down. Some place where no one would see him, there, behind the horticulturalist's workplace, no, here, in the bushes, on a tree trunk, a stump, the ground would be all right, the clammy, musty smelling earth. He adjusted his back against a tree and pulled his knees up under his chin.

First nothing at all was going on in his mind, except a small triumph over downing Molkenboer, probably brought about by a nagging pain in his right hand. To his surprise he laughed aloud. He was startled by his own voice. What had he laughed about so much yesterday? Louise and the gardener. The exorbitant reward for his services. What services actually? She wouldn't pay him for other than soil science expertise, would she? How old was that young man? He could be her son. No, he couldn't. But that made no difference. Was his wife having an affair with her horticulturalist, and was he getting paid for this in extra under-the-counter money? He couldn't believe it. Louise would never do something like that. He would. After the fire. After the burnt offering of patient Van Raai. But that was different. Women didn't do such things. Louise and he were comrades. What they had gone through together was so much, so special—you couldn't share that with someone else. Not she. That chill secret they never talked about was something only between the two of them. He had always thought that. Perhaps nonsense. The gynecologist knew it. The urologist. The adoption center. That slime ball Molkenboer seemed to know that there were problems. Had been. With whom did Louise talk? She didn't talk. He thought. She had sat on a terrace with Ineke Tordoir. Albert's behavior had been paternalistic and devious. Did everyone know without him being aware? He wasn't a fool. He was trained in observing, his reality check was all right. Albert supported him. Molkenboer was afraid of his boss. Louise was faithful to him. That's how it was.

When all this was over, the two of them really should go on vacation again, walk in the mountains, deserted, white, in the thin air. Twenty years ago they had walked high in the Pyrenees, silent, disappointment and despair pulling on their shoulders like heavy knapsacks. Against the steep north slope of the mountain a massive clump of ice stretched down for several hundred yards; that was the icebox for the hot hinterland. In a walking guide he had read how ice carriers set out from the foot of that mountain to bring cooling to the palaces of Foix, of Pamiers, of Toulouse. They would tie the rough-hewn ice slabs on their backs, protected by a sheepskin, and start to walk. How had they felt, what did they think on the way? How had they persevered? Just like Louise and he, bent under a cold burden that with every mile penetrated deeper into their marrow. He had calculated: this many steps to that crossing, that many to the next river. He had set goals for himself and had attained them. Order. Power. But she? Had she stayed right behind him, obediently following in his footsteps? Or had she let her icy burden melt, had she thrown off the stinking, smelly sheepskin and jumped away among the rocks, with a young shepherd? Was he alone?

Suddenly he was cold, and when he tried to get up too quickly, everything turned black before his eyes. For a moment, the smell of rotting leaves bothered him, the aimless sitting had made him faint and he was disgusted by his damp, clammy clothes. Slowly he walked to his office.

"They all left peacefully," said Alice when he entered his room. She was dragging a heavy vacuum cleaner behind her.

"I decided to do some vacuuming. It looked awful. Now it's spic and span again."

"Thank you," said Nico. He marched off to the bathroom and slammed the door behind him. Water. Warmth. He let the stream splash against his chilled back. For a long time.

With wet hair he sat down at his desk and pulled the schedule toward him. Alice came in with a stack of fax papers in her hands.

"The fire department has not yet given permission to enter the area. The investigation hasn't been completed."

She tapped against her teeth with a pen.

"Shall I call off that architect? Otherwise he'll come for nothing this afternoon. And the inspection staff has called; they want to have a meeting fairly soon. About the fire. The claims assessors were here yesterday. They were shown around by Building and Management. Are you going to Mr. Van Raai's funeral? A wreath has been taken care of. Could you say a few words?"

"Stop for a minute, Alice," he said with a sigh. "Why can't I go to the site of the fire with the architect? And when can I? That man has rushed to make a design for the floor plan; I want to proceed. Do *you* see an investigative team of the fire department? *I* don't. We have to postpone our plans, and they do nothing. You arrange it—call the fire chief, call the architect, make a new appointment. Just as long as it's quick."

"The Head of Training also wants an appointment with you, preferably right away. It could be this afternoon before you have to go to the Social Services office."

He rubbed his eyes, stretched his legs, pushed away the schedule. All day long he would have to listen to reproachful, suspicious voices; he would have to restrain himself, shelve his plans indefinitely, control himself, concentrate on what was attainable, excuse himself, bend over backwards—no. Impossible. He couldn't.

"Cancel everything, Alice. I have other plans."

"But how can you possibly? Everyone wants to speak with you!"

"An executive secretary knows how it's done. That's you."

He stood up and passed her with a brief smile. On her desk, in the room next to his, the telephone rang. She picked it up breathing heavily, bending clumsily across the table.

"Oh, Mr. Tordoir, yes, he's here, I'll put you through!"

Nico shook his head and waved the phone aside with a dismissive gesture as he walked through the hall. He could hear her helpless chatter until he let the glass door fall closed behind him.

He was misunderstood, accused, and persecuted by people whom he had considered neutral or even sympathetic co-workers. Abandoned and betrayed by his friend, his child, his wife. Steady, not so melodramatic, he thought, reining himself in, you can get used to everything. Two questions: what is reality and what can you do? Based on that you determine the state of possibilities.

The thinking exercises were liberating. You see, he thought, despair is pointless, a useless burden. I've got to leave these grounds for a moment. Drink a beer in the village. He headed for the village center, over the bicycle path next to the busy highway. Honking motorbikes made him jump aside, heavy trucks loaded with flowers spit dirty gas fumes in his face. Continue walking. Count steps. Know the goal.

"Doctor! Doctor!"

A stocky woman stood on the strip of grass between the bicycle path and the roadway. She wore a sweater with stains, a pleated skirt that hung unevenly and slippers on her bare feet. She clasped a large, straw shopping basket against her chest. Behind the thick glasses he saw her friendly eyes.

"Mrs. Van Overeem! Where are you going?"

"Just crossing the street. I'm looking for the sidewalk."

Two bicycles at top speed grazed Mrs. Van Overeem's rear end.

"They give you a fright. You're not allowed to walk here," said the woman.

Resolutely, she took to the road, without looking right or left. Nico grabbed her arm with two hands and yanked her to him. The heavy body staggered, fell against him, threw him off balance.

"That's certainly not allowed," said the woman. She looked at him, disappointed.

"You're not allowed to cross here," he said curtly. "You're not watching for traffic."

"But I have to go shopping! For the ward! There's no more coffee creamer! What will happen if I don't do it? Well, Doctor Van der Doelen?"

"Calm down, we'll find a solution."

He grabbed her tightly under the arm and tried to make her turn around. Unyielding, impossible to get moving. The woman kept peering at the other side of the road.

"Mrs. Van Overeem, they're waiting for you. With the coffee. We have to go."

"Coffee creamer!"

"You'll get it from me. If you come with me now. Please."

He felt the resolve flow out of her. She had sweat stains under her arms; he sniffed the rather sour smell with revulsion and curiosity. Slowly they walked together to the gate. Every beginning is difficult, he thought; the patients' responsibility for their own social circumstances, but what could have possessed Erik to send such a woman out onto the highway? No, Erik has been at home since the fire: nervous exhaustion. There should be a symposium about step-by-step planning, otherwise everyone just goes and does whatever they please.

They weren't getting anywhere. The slippers dragged over the asphalt, and he had a lot of difficulty keeping his walking partner to a straight course. Every time he looked at her he saw her face distort in a grimace that looked like a smile. Her mouth hung open a little and she drooled slightly from the effort. The gate was still a distance away.

He was going to sue that garden boy. Fraud, extortion, swindle? That skillful lawyer from the Board of Trustees would probably be able to help him. His money back, that was the least he had the right to. And Louise, he would reprimand her too. A discussion tonight. Or perhaps not? Better be silent about it. Look for hickeys on her neck, letters in her desk drawer. He felt the blood rise to his head. To think that she'd got involved with such a nincompoop, a product of a martial arts school, a common crook. And he was supposed to be happy that she assumed responsibility for that shitty garden. Run a bulldozer through it and then dump gravel everywhere, that's what he was going to do. An act. He was sick to death of these unspoken reproaches. If a child threatened to blow her final examination because of nerves or a needless lack of confidence, you as her father had the right to take action. Or perhaps not? And he was an expert to boot. Offer structure and make demands—that makes insecure people improve. He couldn't help it that she had packed a small sports bag and had disappeared. Louise hadn't offered an alternative; she should have been happy that he'd intervened. What else should he have done? That passive resistance, that gloomy act, that bending under fate—I'm fed up with it. Letting herself be consoled by the gardener, against payment of large sums of money—how was it possible? Of course he'd been all over her in the shed with those muscular arms. A body full of hormones. Flattered that an older woman with nice hips had fallen for him. Revolting.

When they had shuffled through the gate, Mrs. Van Overeem started on again about the coffee creamer.

"I can't come back without it. That's the new regime. I have to do it myself."

"You've got to stop now," he said sternly. "Coffee creamer is very bad. It makes you fat. We're going to take it out of the food choices. Tell that to the social services manager. And it's nasty as well."

Mrs. Van Overeem now seemed overcome with confusion and threatened to come to a total standstill. Nico renewed his grip on her arm and started pulling vigorously.

"Look, there's your ward already! We're going to discuss it, come on."

"No, I don't live there at all," the woman said, surprised.

"Yes you do. You've been living there since the fire. I'm sure of it."

"Yes, lots of fire, terrible wasn't it," she said. She began to sob hard. Nico waved to a figure behind the door of the pavilion. He saw an arm that waved back and right away started to despair. Come now, please come! Then the door opened and Eva came out. He exhaled.

Together they took the flushed patient to the living room.

"How are you?" asked Eva. "You don't look very well, can I do something for you?"

"Just do something for these patients of yours," he said bluntly. "Watch that they don't run away, for example. I plucked her out from under a car."

She placed Mrs. Van Overeem at the table where several patients were rocking back and forth, staring into the distance. No one had a comment about the return of the fugitive, no one was interested in milk for the coffee.

Eva walked to the office and pulled off her apron. He remained standing in the doorway and looked at her.

"You can do something for me," he said. "Come with me. I have to get out, away, I'm suffocating here."

Without a word she followed him outside.

He felt his jacket. Good, wallet. Eva had already jumped in. Quickly he turned the car out of the parking lot, avoiding a look at the entrance of the main building, where in a moment Alice would step outside furious, where Albert had perhaps already arrived to suspend him, the police to arrest him for assault and battery, the fire department to bring charges against him. The enormous power of the motor thrilled him and he steered the car off the grounds like a tank.

Once on the highway he picked up speed and chose the left lane, easily passing trucks and brightly colored small cars. Through the dark-tinted windshield the sky seemed bright gray-white, as if that morning's sunny spring weather no longer existed. Thanks to the air-conditioning it was pleasantly cool. He kept the windows closed; he wanted the car to be a closed domain without influence from outside, with its own laws. Just as he expected his patients to place themselves outside their disease, to stop looking for backgrounds and explanations and to concentrate solely on a healthy schedule and healing acts, in the same way he abandoned reflection and concentrated on the few cubic feet of space inside the silver shell of the Volvo. With every vanishing mile he left behind the runaway child, the unfaithful wife, the lecherous gardener and the traitors whom he had considered colleagues. Their offences, their reproach, and their anger evaporated and lost menace and meaning. If you really wanted to, you could force your thoughts to remain inside the safe enclosure of the useful and the manageable. If you just wanted to intensely enough.

Through the thin fabric of his summer trousers he felt the cool leather of the seat. Except for a soft hissing, it was quiet in the car. No music. Without any effort his foot rested on the gas pedal, his hand on the steering wheel, his head against the seatback. Nothing refused service, nothing was obstructive, nothing was wrong.

He looked sideways and saw Eva's profile. A smooth, unblemished face, turned attentively to the view. The gray skirt lay uncreased on her suntanned knees. She had placed her shoes neatly on the floor and rested her bare feet against the map shelf under the glove compartment. She looked peaceful and content.

Near Schiphol they zoomed underneath an airplane that was lifting off. Where were they going? Antwerp, she had said, tapping on the knobs of that idiotic orientation device next to his steering wheel. Fine, excellent. But then along the coast. At any rate Zealand. He wanted to see borders and barriers, locks and dikes. He wanted to show her that it was possible to master and control the most destructive forces, that people could solve any problem as long as they thought carefully and didn't let themselves be carried along by their emotions to areas where reason is wasted. For centuries people had tried to hold the water back with prayer, had wanted to change the character of the sea. It didn't succeed until people could recognize the capacity of the sea and based on that, were able to develop a flood barrier.

"Have you ever seen the Delta Works?"

She smiled and shook her head. The thick, matte blond hair moved over her shoulder. He would drive from island to island, effortlessly, over bridges and locks, over dangerous gray water where people used to labor in narrow ships, fighting the tide that pulled on them.

Hugging the dunes, through the stiff woods that were there to tie down and hold back the sand of the dunes. Over the dikes that resisted the sea when the sand was washed away. He wanted to show her a planned landscape. They got out in a very quiet village. There was a café in a centuries-old house on a small square. The chairs stood on the rounded cobblestones of the pavement; they sat down facing south and looked out on a canal with its small merchant houses, a brick bridge, and a water gate.

He looked for a long time at her ankles, at the flawless bump of the bone, at the blue marking of the veins, at the cream color of the skin.

Later they walked around to look at the church, the ruins of the old cloister, and the twisting and turning small streets behind it. He took her hand, her firm, young hand. His right foot longed again for the pedals.

He tore across the dam and found his way straight through the green countryside to Vlissingen. She had to see the boulevard before evening fell because nowhere else was the sky as lilac and purple as there. He led her to the jetty, and they saw how the sun colored the wild bank of clouds. Afterwards, a mist crept out of the water and he noticed that she was shivering. He pressed her against him and hung his jacket over her shoulders and folded his warm arms around her.

They ate in front of an enormous window through which they saw tankers and freighters with strange names sail past, surprisingly close to the shore. He pointed out to her the yellow pilot boat which sailed up to a ship at great speed and came alongside it. She peered intently at the ship and saw the pilot, just a speck, climbing against the gray hull. Long before he had reached the top, the small pilot boat was already tearing across the water. He told her that the pilot took over the command. The captain had to stand by and watch how the pilot guided the ship through the treacherous water. She squeezed his hand; she smiled.

The sun had set completely when they were finished with dinner. The sky and the water were black, and there was no moon. They walked back up the boulevard and saw the lights of the ships and the beams of the lighthouse beacons moving across the shining river, over the sea in the distance. The car traveled over the empty roads to Antwerp. On traffic circles and median strips daffodils stood at the height of their bloom, with wide-open calyxes and bracts folded back, as if they yearned for sunlight. It was night.

He called the hotel from the car and reserved a room with a view of the courtyard. He was welcome, the owner said, the car could go in the garage, he would be there directly, after all, it wasn't busy on the road. Nico smiled, it was as if the language affirmed that everything was different now, that new rules applied here, different from the region where he spoke and understood standard Dutch. He placed his hand on Eva's thigh and caressed the skin along the edge of her skirt with his fingers. Explain nothing, he thought, no stories, no justifications. Not: my wife doesn't understand me; she's run away with the gardener. No questions. Not: do you do this often, don't you have a boyfriend, is your father still alive, are you in love with me. I'm ageless. He steered the car deftly into the inner city. Delighted, Eva sat looking at the façades. She had placed her hand on his. He wanted to show her everything, the secret small squares, the medieval alleys, the raised promenades along the Scheldt. He wanted to buy her clothes, marked with enormous, unmanageable prices in Belgian money, perfume, jewelry, purses. He wanted to feed her fish, oysters, flinty white wine. Black truffles and white chocolate bonbons. He wanted to take care of her. She would lack for nothing. She knew that, she appreciated it and would be grateful to him. He would make her happy.

He found the hotel in the narrow street and for a moment he felt the familiar irritation when the door of the hotel garage appeared to be closed—as if Louise, Albert, Molkenboer, and the gardener appeared hissing with indignation from behind the partitions in his head to reprimand him and to condemn him. Everyone was out to cross him and to frustrate him. Even here! His heart rhythm quickened and he started breathing heavily. Then the solid figure of the hotel owner appeared and pushed open the door, which rattled softly, revealing a sea of space where he could choose any parking place. He shook his head to get rid of the thoughts. Nothing was the matter. It was good. They were there.

The window open, please, but the curtains preferably closed. He could do without the sky with its stars as pinholes; the white square of this room and this bed were enough for him. He had ordered up wine, and lay stretched-out on the pale sheets, balancing the glass on his chest. Water splashed in the bathroom, Eva's clothes lay on the chair. The threatening phantoms in his head had been silenced. Now came the night.

He started awake in the total darkness. Groping, he discovered the edges of the bed, the unfamiliar carpet under his feet, a closed door, a door that could be opened. In the bathroom he leaned against the wall, sweating, sick with fear. The mirror reflected his face, a lined face with red blotches and dark bags under the eyes. Slowly he widened the opening to the room. The beam of light fell on the bed where a child lay, a girl who had clasped her slender arms around the pillow. A child.

For at least an hour he sat on the lid of the toilet and massaged his head. When the trembling of his calves lessened, he washed himself with cold water. He slipped into the room and got dressed. He took all the cash out of his wallet and placed it on the bed. Carefully he moved to the door. He tiptoed even in the hall. The night porter took him to the garage, he drove out of the street, out of the city, into the darkness. He stopped his car alongside the road, leaned with his head and arms against the steering wheel, and began to cry.

Chapter seven

The fact that he didn't come home at the end of the day hadn't particularly alarmed her. Frequently she didn't know if he had a commitment, an engagement or a meeting; she simply didn't hear what he said or she forgot immediately. First she waited before starting the cooking, later she decided not to do it at all. In front of the television she drank a glass of milk and ate a bag of chips. She couldn't stand the babble of the newscaster, so she turned off the sound and looked at the pointlessly moving mouth, the meaningless husk of the words. It was still light outside, she could still go into the garden for a moment. The newscaster imploded into a lighted spot on a black surface.

The mole had been busy again under the grass plot. She started to dig away the raised sand piles. She knew that you had to push empty bottles into them; then the wind would start up and create a terrifying chord in the mole tunnels that would paralyze the mole. She kicked the holes closed with her heel and threw soil over them. Whoever held out longest was the winner. Wessel had mentioned poison and traps; he had wanted to go out immediately to the garden center to purchase the weapons, but she would have none of it and insisted on offering the mole a fair fight. She would have liked to have enticed him to choose his domicile among the pine trees: so many roots to gnaw to pieces, so much loose sand to throw around, so much space, so much peace and quiet. But the blind animal had chosen her grass plot.

Suddenly she couldn't stand the garden. She closed the kitchen door and walked through the gate. Cold evening air sank to the ground, the bicycle path glowed bright gray in the twilight. From a distance, she looked at her house, where she, just like the mole, kept returning because she didn't know any better. Walk. Unwind the soles of her feet on the ground, fists balled in the pockets of her coat. Dying dark blue blackberries, tufts of beach grass, dune sand. Something chafed against her heel. Sand. Sand that pricks, irritates, and hurts. Nasty, sneaky sand.

Nonsense. Sand does nothing, it only is. The fact that I think that sand is pricking me is a trick of the verb. Sand lets itself be carried along in the shoe, but I'm the one who does something: I feel pain and become angry. I could also not react, then the sand would be powerless. She climbed the last row of dunes and saw the empty beach. Footsteps, paw prints, sandcastles had all been wiped away by the sea; at the horizon the sky was colored pale yellow by the no longer visible sun. Slowly she walked back home.

Dark windows. No silver car in the driveway. Did she want him to come home that much? His absence was like the sand: as annoying as she thought it was. Suddenly she was seized by a restless thirst for action, and with trembling fingers she groped in her coat pocket for the key which she tried to stuff into the lock of the kitchen door, stomping her feet impatiently. Inside, she threw down her coat and kicked off her shoes. She stormed up the stairs and began to strip the bed. She shook out blankets and comforters on the balcony, breathing heavily, with big gestures. From the corner of her eye she saw the woman next door look up surprised. She looked back fixedly, without a greeting, before, covered by the mountain of bedding, she stepped back into the bedroom between the glass doors. She stuffed the dirty laundry into the hamper and made the bed tightly with fragrant sheets.

She found no peace and quiet at the kitchen table. She noticed that she was listening intently to what was happening outside. It wasn't much, only some leaves of the garden trees rustling together in the slight evening breeze, the neighbor who closed the window, and the silence: the lack of engine sounds, a closing car door, the squeaking of a door handle.

Abruptly she got up. The dishwasher had to be emptied, the dishes placed in the cupboard, the plates where they belonged, the cutlery in the drawers. She flung the forks forcefully into their compartment, grabbed carelessly for the knives and cut herself in the fleshy underside of her fingers. She sucked the blood from the wound, furious.

The glass salad bowl slipped out of her hands and shattered into pieces on the floor. She cursed. Then she ran to the hall closet and pulled the vacuum cleaner into the kitchen. Licking her injured hand, she began to vacuum up the glass splinters; they rattled tinkling into the hose. The motor of the vacuum cleaner whined; the undercarriage crunched over the floor. When she finally turned off the machine it was ominously quiet all of a sudden.

Drink, she could drink. That was also good against the pain. First stick band-aids on her fingers. Blood spots on the scissors that she used to cut them to size, biting her lips in order not to scream. With the left hand clumsily maneuver the sticky ends in place, hurriedly, with too much force. Exaggeratedly calm she took the gin bottle from the refrigerator and carried it to the living room. She walked back again to get a glass. Now sit down on the sofa. Pour carefully, don't spill. With the wrong hand bring the glass to her mouth. Feel the sharp, stinging, but numbing liquid against her lips. Silence.

She could call the hospital. There should be a night porter who picked up the phone. What should she say? Where is my husband, he hasn't come home. Inconceivable, she wouldn't do that. But why not? Perhaps the porter would say that there had been a meeting with the Board of Trustees and that they had gone out to eat. It'll probably run late ma'am; just wait, the doctor will come soon. No, it felt as if, were she to phone, she'd be handing over any power that she still had. Don't do it.

And the police? Has there been an accident with a silver Volvo with my husband in it? Oh, my dear lady, he's been gone for only one evening? Those are usually accidents of another sort, do call back tomorrow if you haven't heard anything. Raging with powerless anger and humiliation, she would slam the receiver down. If something had happened, if the Volvo had come to a standstill, bent around an enormous beech tree, if Nico, crushed and with a broken neck, was hanging against his airbag, people would certainly check on it, even in the middle of the night. Then the police, with gloved fingers, would search in Nico's pockets for a driver's license or a credit card; then she would be called or picked up by a serious inspector who would ask her to identify the body.

She shook her head and stood up. She'd drunk enough. She wanted to go to bed, the night had to pass, the strange thoughts had to go, and if no one could help her with that, she'd have to do it herself. Despite last night's hilarious reaction, he was probably angry about the money, incensed at her naiveté, and wanted to punish her by making her worried. She would put on a brave front. Nothing was wrong. She could call Wessel; she could simply inquire what exactly had happened with the sums she had slipped him. She should have insisted on getting his phone number—he was never there, he said, so many people lived there, a chaotic house, students and such, messages weren't passed on, it was no use. After all, he came every week, she didn't need to call him at all. Reluctantly he had written a number on a scrap of paper. He's ashamed, she had thought, he doesn't want his friends to see him as a gardener, he is embarrassed to be summoned to the telephone by an older person; he's still a child.

It lay in the drawer where she kept her money. Determinedly she punched in the number. Although it was close to midnight, she didn't hesitate.

"Hello," said a girl's voice with a nasal sound, "just a moment, just let me get the ashtray…"

"I'm looking for Wessel ten Cate."

"Oh," said the girl. It became silent on the other end. Then she heard crackling crashes, as if the receiver were dangling on the cord and kept banging against the wall. In between that a conversation could be heard vaguely; the girl shouted short phrases with a questioning tone.

"Are you still there? There's no one here with that name."

"But he lives there! Are you sure?"

"Oh yes," said the girl with her pinched voice. "I asked. You have the wrong number."

She hung up. Wrong number. Perhaps he had accidentally written down a wrong number. Or deliberately. Maybe he used to live there, had moved, was living somewhere else, with a girlfriend, with Maj maybe. Maybe they were squandering her twenty-five thousand guilders together. In Paris.

For an instant she felt a strange relief, as if she had traced both fugitives and had lodged them someplace in safety. Satisfaction. Well done. She had done nothing but blunder, commit stupidites. She'd given away a fortune to a perfect stranger. Let a daughter disappear. Given a man cause to despise her. The gin bottle belonged in the refrigerator. The doors should be locked but not bolted; he could still come. The light above the stove should stay on. And now up the stairs with her hand on the banisters.

She hesitated about taking a shower; she longed for the warmth but couldn't face the splashing and roar that would drown all other sounds. She washed herself at the sink, brushed her hair and her teeth. She didn't look at herself in the mirror, and in the dark bedroom she crawled between the fresh sheets. She lay down on Nico's side where the telephone was.

When she woke up, she didn't know where she was. She reached toward Nico but felt emptiness. The bed ended. There was no Nico. She was alone. She sat straight up and pulled her knees toward her. With her head on her knees she reflected. The mobile phone, he had his mobile phone with him. Stupid that she hadn't thought of that right away. Naked, she walked downstairs to get her date book out of her purse; back upstairs she sat down on her bed and looked up the number. *Paying close attention she entered the long row of numbers.* The ringing stopped after three times. She held her breath.

"This mobile phone is temporarily not in use. Please try again later," said a metallic voice.

Carefully, she replaced the receiver. She switched off the lamp and pulled the sheet over her face. Morning was bound to come very soon.

It seemed to be a normal Friday morning when she sat in the kitchen. She didn't have to be at school; time was of no importance. The sky was heavily overcast, but it didn't rain. The grass plot looked as it did yesterday, the mole had kept quiet last night. She contemplated working in the garden but didn't really feel like it. It was better to go away and come back home again than to remain waiting inside the house. She would go bicycling, she decided. But first eat something, and drink coffee, and open all the curtains.

The telephone rang when she was pulling up the Venetian blinds in Nico's study. She sat down on his desk chair and picked up the phone.

"Louise, this is Albert. Please excuse me for disturbing you so early, but I'd like to speak with Nico. They said that he wasn't in the hospital yet; that's why I thought: I'll try him at home. Or is he on his way?"

On his way, she thought, on his way. Yes, that's probably true. I have to say something; my throat is tight.

"Hello! Louise? Are you still there?"

She coughed, cleared her throat and swallowed. The words didn't come. Strange, for the other her silence was an invitation to make a sound. What a nice voice he had, the irritation was barely noticeable.

"Were you very upset by yesterday's events? You understand

that I have to speak with Nico; I'm afraid that it's more or less an official talk; I'm telephoning in my official capacity. Can you please call him?"

She stood up, it made no sense at all, but she was standing. Did she want to stick her head around the door and call out Nico's name into the hall?

"Albert, he's not here."

To her surprise her voice sounded cool and businesslike.

"He hasn't been home all night. I don't know where he is. His telephone isn't working. For that matter, I don't know what happened. I don't know what I should be upset about."

"I'll be right over," said Albert. "Stay where you are, I'll be with you in half an hour."

She heard the click when the conversation was finished and remained standing with the receiver in her hand. On the desk lay disorganized stacks of magazines, notes, reports. A sea of paper, and she stood on the beach. If she didn't dash away fast she would sink into quicksand.

She welcomed him and brought him into the living room; they sat down on the sofa, turned toward each other diagonally. She was silent.

Albert took off his glasses and polished them with his handkerchief. She waited. He put his glasses back on, looked outside and coughed behind his hand. Then he looked at her.

"You don't know how unpleasant this is for me, Louise. I would have preferred to sit here for another reason. But this is how it is. I'll be clear, that's best."

She crossed her legs and turned her face to him. Despite the ominous atmosphere of the conversation, she found it pleasant not to be alone, nice to listen and to look at the expression on his face.

"You know that I wanted to speak to you about your husband the other day because I was worried. I couldn't be more explicit at the time, but now an emergency situation has arisen which allows me to be released from my pledge of secrecy. Our first priority must be to find Nico again."

She nodded. His formal language was helping her to assume her familiar observing attitude. She would register which things he mentioned and how they were related to one another. The substantives, the verbs. The color of the adjectives. She straightened her back.

"First I have to tell you a number of things, however unpleasant that may be. It is clear that Nico is under enormous pressure; he is no longer himself. There was an unpleasant conflict with the employee-management council about his policies, and above all, about the tempo of this work. That's to be expected, and in itself it isn't serious, but yesterday there was an escalation. A fight broke out; Nico knocked Jaap Molkenboer down. Molkenboer has been admitted to the hospital with a broken nose and various injuries. He has reported it. The police are looking for Nico in connection with assault and battery. I'm sorry, Louise."

He touched her wrist for a moment. She saw how his hand lay on her arm. White fingers on a tanned skin. She didn't like Molkenboer; she found him hypocritical and devious. It didn't surprise her at all that Nico had beaten him up. Did she disapprove? That was not under discussion, she had to listen.

"In addition there is the problem of the fire. The safety measures were totally inadequate. The alarm didn't function, and no sprinkler system had been installed because the building was due to be demolished. Moreover, it was found that the staff locked rooms where patients slept, contrary to the rules. You know that a patient died as a result of that. Of course Nico didn't have a hand in all these matters, but as director he is officially responsible. The fire department has temporarily closed off the area for an investigation and wants to question Nico. Nico has refused this, and that is harmful for the organization. Yesterday I had emergency talks with my fellow board members, and regrettably we had to make the decision to suspend Nico. Immediately."

She looked at the floor. He had small feet; she had never been struck by that before. Nicely polished shoes, certainly, but childishly small. What he said had to get through to her; she mustn't let herself get distracted. Suspended. Small feet, large words. She felt disappointment and annoyance. What was he babbling on about rules, safety requirements, responsibility? As if Nico could help it that the pavilions were collapsing, that the required measures were not consistent with reality, that the employee-management council was populated with vindictive obstructionists. Nico had done his best; he had made a supreme effort. There always had to be one person with a vision, someone who led the way and gave direction. That was Nico. The others hung onto the reins and held him back. She smiled in spite of herself when she thought of him with his silly bike cap, pulling a cart filled with heavy therapists.

"I fear that there is nothing to laugh about," said Albert.

She froze. He was a millstone around Nico's neck. He was biased. He went by other people's stories and accepted them unthinkingly. The blood rose to her cheeks, and she breathed deeply, opened her mouth. No, she told herself, calm now! No expression or reaction.

"Isn't it strange that you move straight to suspension before even talking with Nico?"

After all, I'm not crazy, she thought. I've seen so many quarrels and conflicts at school; I recognize a panic solution when I see one. What a cowardly game—point out a scapegoat before you've done a solid investigation, offer a protagonist to satisfy the choir.

"If you think that he's under severe strain, wouldn't it be obvious to have him go on sick leave?"

Exasperating that she still put her comment in the form of a question. She should be dictating, positing, ordering. With exclamation marks. Retract that suspension! Listen to my husband! Look at your own responsibility!

Albert was silent. He bent forward and let his head rest on his hands. She couldn't see his face. Suddenly her combativeness left her, and doubt and anxiety arose with force.

"There's something else," said Albert. "I find this terribly difficult, but I have to discuss it with you. There's something else."

"Yes?"

"This morning I talked on the phone with Alice, the executive secretary."

The spic and span lady, she thought, from Duress and Company. He's going to tell me that she brought charges of intimidation against him. She sniffed.

"She said that yesterday, after the unfortunate incident with Molkenboer, Nico drove away. He was not alone."

She looked at him questioning, her head raised.

"He had a girl with him in the car. They drove away together."

Maj she thought. He has reconciled with Maj. He looked for her, found her, took her with him. Soon they'll come home and everything will be fine. She had to control the impulse to jump up and start walking through the room. He can get lost now, he's said enough. Maj!

But Albert continued to speak.

"An employee," he said. "A young woman who worked on the ward where the fire was. A promising, talented trainee. There are rumors, unfortunately, that Nico and she—recently …well, from a reliable source I found out that they—an affair, that they're having an affair. I regret this more than I can say. For you. But also for Nico. I never would have expected that of him. Naturally, I'd first want to hear his side. But I'm afraid that we may not be able to get around this. She hasn't appeared for work either this morning, so it looks like they've gone away together."

Albert fell silent awkwardly. During his account he had stared straight ahead, now he turned around and looked at her.

"Did you know about it? Or is it a surprise for you? Terrible that we have to talk about this now. To be honest, I'm rather shocked by it. Of course it can't be allowed—a director having a sexual relationship with an employee—it goes against all ethics. It carries the penalty of dismissal, although we shouldn't get ahead of the matter. Did you expect anything like that, do you understand it?"

The gym shoes, the bicycling compulsion, the energy, the

weight loss, the much too youthful cap. The long workdays, the disinterest in what she was actually doing. Yes, of course she should have known it. It was her own fault; she had no interest in him anymore, never wanted to go away with him, and was always somber. Not attractive enough. A trainee. A promising trainee. She didn't doubt for a moment that it was true. It made sense; it explained everything. Had she paid attention, she would have known.

She leaned back with her head against the sofa. Her hands lay limp against her thighs. She started crying very softly, with closed eyes.

Time passed. Albert reached in his pants pocket, coughed, and handed her a folded handkerchief, which she pressed against her eyes. It was still warm. The crying intensified, she sobbed next to the silent man who had shared his body warmth so quietly with her. The temperature of his thighs conveyed what his words couldn't.

She blew her nose and began to talk, without purpose and without plan. In unbroken sentences that rolled effortlessly into the room she described how the past half year had been, how Nico had fought his powerlessness by burying himself in his work, how she had numbed herself with her unachievable garden plans. And what had taken place *before* that: the nightly homework sessions, the expectations, the exhortations that degenerated into shouting matches, the steadily approaching final school examination—all of which brought on frenzies of impatience in Nico, resignation in her, and terror in the child. The small sports bag that had disappeared when they returned from the movies one evening. The empty room with the narrow bed, neatly made. The deserted desk with books and magazines in small, neat stacks.

"Of course it was always amiss. She was elusive. Do you want to do hockey, I would ask, volleyball, jazz ballet? She'd nod and disappear off to the field with her hockey stick fastened to the bike. If we asked her if she wanted to stop hockey, she nodded too, and remained at home. She did what we expected of her. Until it no longer worked.

"Why didn't we ask for help? Because nothing was wrong

according to Nico. Once I said something about it to Molkenboer, during one of the management dinners. I should never have done it; I had drunk too much. He laughed at me; he didn't see a problem and advised me to go into therapy myself. I didn't feel up to that."

"I don't understand," said Albert. "After all, Nico is a psychiatrist himself, couldn't he see that something had to be done?"

"If something had to be done, it meant he had failed," she said derisively. "So he saw nothing. He couldn't shape or change her with his methods. Failure is written on her forehead. Her whole existence is an indictment. He can't stand her being here."

She pushed the handkerchief against her mouth, as if she wanted to smother the fierceness of her voice. She stared outside, where the cloud cover started to break up and the trees bent under the rising wind. Nothing to lose, she thought. Nothing. I can say everything.

"She is an adopted child. We couldn't have children ourselves."

She giggled and pulled her skirt over her knees coquettishly.

"Do you want coffee, Albert? I've completely forgotten to offer you anything."

Albert shook his head.

"What was the reason?" he asked earnestly.

She shrugged her shoulders.

"Tests. Awful. I thought that it would be my fault, but that was only partially true. A blocked Fallopian tube because of a neglected infection. The other side still worked. I'm half good."

A forced, joyless smile escaped her.

"Nico had himself examined at the same time. We've always been for equality. And what did the urologist find? Infertile seed. Unbelievable. We didn't believe it. But it was true. Dead sperm. Without apparent cause. Simply dead instead of simply alive. We didn't have to quarrel about whose fault it was.

"It became a crisis between us. He couldn't accept it. My gynecologist proposed donor insemination, but I knew for sure that Nico wouldn't be able to handle it. A baby crawling around in our house that I'd received from someone else, and Nico pleased with that? I couldn't imagine it. We had to be equal, equally powerless, equally failures. So it was adoption; it was Maj."

Albert got up and walked to the window with his hands clasped behind his back.

"I never knew anything about this," he said softly.

Her voice sounded equally subdued.

"It was no secret. Everyone could find out, but no one knew it. If you knew it, you still didn't know it. Of course we talked about it with Maj, the way it's supposed to be done. She seemed to take note of it because we did no more than that: notify her. Above all not show that you feel anything. We felt nothing either. A perfect, icy little family. You should go, Albert. Please go, now."

Blundering, he said goodbye, first in the living room, hurried, excusing himself that he hadn't gone yet, and then once more in the hall where she had already opened the door and was waiting with arms crossed until he walked clumsily down the steps.

"I'll contact you as soon as I know anything," he said.

Four inches from his stiff back the door banged shut.

She was still holding the handkerchief, crumpled into a ball. She saw him trudge down the driveway and thought: the party's over. The memory of one of Maj's birthdays overwhelmed her—how old could she have been, five, six? They had hung streamers, decorated her chair, baked a cake, lit the candles. She had made a festive dinner and they had sung. When they brought her to bed, the child had asked: when does the party start? Suddenly she had realized that she, Nico and Maj were inexperienced skaters on thin ice, busy balancing, afraid to fall, fearful of clinging to one another. There had been no party, they'd only pretended.

She was on the point of leaving and at the door when the phone rang.

"Hello, this is Louise Van der Doelen."

She heard a silence, interspersed with static crackling, a firmament with small sounds here and there.

"Hello," she shouted loudly and stomped the floor impatiently with her hiking shoes.

"Louise? It's me."

"Oh."

"Can you hear me? There's so much static!"

"I hear you."

But I am going to listen, she thought. She had a choice: either she would let her knees buckle, pull a chair toward her and sit down trembling, or she would set her feet slightly apart, straighten her back and feel the buttoned coat like a sturdy harness around herself. It was as if she looked at herself anxiously, curious how this woman in walking clothes would behave.

"It's not good. I'm in Belgium. I started driving last night; I don't know where I am. I'm so sorry, I didn't want it, but it happened nonetheless."

She was silent, straight, supporting the hand that held the receiver with her other arm, feet apart firmly planted on the floor.

"I went away with a woman. Just like that. Yesterday. Things were getting too much for me. I'm sorry. It means nothing; you know that, don't you?

"The police are looking for you," she said abruptly. "And the fire department. And Albert Tordoir. You've been suspended. Laid off."

She heard him shout but couldn't understand what he said. The line gurgled like a babbling brook. Fragments of phrases appeared in the empty spaces between the static.

"… not the worst … she did … Maj … a daughter … forgive … the bridge at Willebroek … regret …"

She broke off the connection and stood looking at the telephone with arms akimbo.

When it rang again, she picked up immediately.

"We weren't able to mourn her departure because we could

never grieve about her coming. I did it all wrong. It wasn't fair to her, to you. I want to start anew. I don't care about that job, I care about you. About us."

She didn't know if she understood his words correctly because the sound became gradually weaker and the gurgling began again.

"I want you back, Louise. I want us to really talk, like we used to. I think my battery is running down. Louise? Louise?"

It became quiet, a dead silence, without static or background noises. There was no longer a connection.

She took off her coat and placed her shoes in the hall. With heavy legs, she dragged herself upstairs where she opened the door to Maj's room without hesitating. The afternoon sun fell on the bed with the smoothly pulled pale spread. She closed the door, set the window ajar, and let herself fall on the bed. She fished the pillow from under the spread and folded it double under her head. Reflect. Examine what she actually thought about it. Determine her position. She fell asleep.

Vaguely, in the distance, she heard the telephone ring. It didn't occur to her to get up. The sound stopped and began again practically right away. It didn't concern her. As long as she was in this room, she had nothing to do with the rest of the house. He must have recharged his battery and wanted to continue the planning barrage. Everything would probably be changed again. She closed her eyes and tried to ignore the sound. She pictured Nico, lost in the Flemish countryside, among dilapidated auto workshops and fish and chips stands. She should be furious because he had deceived her. She should feel cast aside and repudiated, set aside for a younger woman. But she felt nothing but an intense fatigue. She should have been glad that he finally offered an opening for talking, that he could grieve about his daughter and that he wanted to say that to her. But she felt a strange indifference. The fact that she herself had given a fortune to Wessel was the only thing that made her really angry. Despite the fanatical ringing she must have fallen asleep again, for when she woke up it was almost dark. The wind had died down, the clouds had joined and a gentle rain was falling. The telephone was silent.

She lay looking at the white rectangle of the ceiling, spotless, perfect. I'm going away from here, away from this house, from this garden, from these terrible dunes, from that miserable sea. Start anew he had said. There was an empty, light gray quiet in her head where small interrogative sentences spun round. Alone? Another job? With Nico? Answers didn't occur to her.

Soon he could be standing in front of the door; it was only a few hours of driving. And then, she'd have to know. He would ring the bell because it wasn't clear if he would be allowed to come in. She had to say it. Her words weighed heaviest, she was in the position to let the scale tip over to her side. Later, years later perhaps, the bill would come and the balance would tip. That's how it went between husband and wife.

The telephone started up again. Slowly she sat up and moved to the edge of the bed. If it could only be done without a scale, if he would come in shortly and say: we're stopping it, we'll no longer compare, we'll no longer assess, we'll no longer make up balances. If the debits and credits could go into the fire, it would become possible to be together again. Perhaps. She had to stop crossing off the bicycling trips against the gardening passion, weighing the trainee against the gardener. If they no longer needed to transform and restructure each other, they could allow what happened to take place, without obfuscation, without distortion.

She stood up and walked out of the room. She left the door open.

She moved as if she were several pounds lighter, with quick and lithe movements she ran around the upper floor. If the telephone would ring now, she would pick up, but it remained quiet in the house. She had claimed the third room for herself as a matter of course and started to pack Maj's hated schoolbooks in cardboard boxes, to strip the bed, to put away the toys. If her daughter ever came back, she should be able to be herself. With parents who were no more than themselves. She stuffed the hockey clothes and the ballet things into a garbage bag. Then the bell rang.

With her heels she gave an extra thump on the wide stair treads as she stormed downstairs. Now!

On the steps stood a policeman who looked at her bare feet. Slowly he lifted his head. He was a middle-aged black man and wore glasses with a gold frame. When he lifted the cap from his head to stick it under his arm, she saw a wreath of grayish white, frizzy hair.

"Mrs. Van der Doelen?"

Dazed, she kept looking at him and didn't react.

"My name is Hendrik Lantzaad. Sergeant Lantzaad. May I come in for a moment? I have a message for you."

Nico. The interrogation. She let go of the door handle and stepped aside.

"My husband isn't here yet."

"I know that, ma'am."

He walked past her into the hall.

"Could we sit down somewhere?" he said over his shoulder. "Go ahead and close the door."

She led the way into the kitchen and showed him Nico's chair. He placed his cap on the table and waited until she sat down. Then he pulled his chair under him and moved close to the edge of the table. He spread his forearms in front of him and bent slightly toward her.

"I have bad news for you. Your husband has had a car accident."

He paused before he continued.

"I'm afraid that your husband has been killed."

It wasn't until then that she saw that the man had an identification card in his hand. Through the plastic cover she saw a reduced version of the dark head with the wreath of curls.

"Ma'am?"

She looked at him.

"First I want to express my sincere condolences."

The sound of his singsong voice came from afar. Yet he was so close that she could easily touch his gray-brown hands.

"You know that your husband was in Belgium?"

She nodded.

"He went off the road, hit a tree and then went into the water. In a canal. At Willebroek. We're waiting for a report from our Belgian colleagues. It happened in the early afternoon. Not much is known about the circumstances. Of course there will be an investigation. I can tell you that there were no oncoming cars, and your husband was probably not driving too fast either. There are still many questions."

He was silent again. It remained quiet for a considerable time.

Then he got up and took a glass from the counter that he rinsed carefully and filled up with cold water. He held it out to her; she had to control the urge to move her mouth toward it and let herself be given water like a child. She lifted her arm and closed her hand around the glass. She drank.

"Is there someone I can call for you? Do you want to go somewhere? Family? A girlfriend? Children?"

She shook her head.

"I'll keep you informed about the developments. It will take a day or two before I will invite you for the formalities. The identification. Transfer of possessions. But I would like to speak with you again tomorrow. Is that all right?"

She nodded again.

"It's not good to be alone after such bad news, I think. But people are different; no one's the same. If you prefer, I'll leave you alone now. Are you sure? I would like to stay with you for a while. I'll write down my telephone number for you, then you can reach me whenever you want."

He took a pen from his breast pocket and wrote a row of numbers on the back of a business card that he then placed in front of her. Then he shook her hand and gently closed the door behind him.

The cemetery was in the middle of an undulating dune landscape. She insisted that the car go no farther than the gate and that she herself cover, step by step, the winding road to the auditorium at the top of the dune. She would have preferred to walk over a grassy dike, in boots, against the wind that would blow tears to the corners of her eyes. But it was calm under the pine trees, and she was wearing black pumps with heels that kept sinking slightly too deep into the sand.

She walked between Albert and Ineke; there was barely space for three people on the narrow path. Ineke had slipped an arm through hers. Her two companions talked softly to each other and held her enclosed with their words.

"Look at the crowd," said Albert. "There is Hein Bruggink. And Molkenboer, out of the hospital. Just in time."

"Do you have a handkerchief?" asked Ineke. "We'll sit next to you. You don't have to do anything. Albert will take care of everything, isn't that right, Albert?"

A long line of people dressed in black crept up to the white building. When she came inside, two young men dashed toward her and took her and her companions into the hall. Three quarters of the chairs were already occupied, and people stood three rows deep on the sides. There was a marble podium. On it stood a coffin.

Slowly they walked to the front, between people who moved aside respectfully and turned toward her. Jaap Molkenboer had a black eye. His nose was packed in a striking plaster construction that was attached to his forehead. Hein and Aleid Bruggink joined them and walked with them to the front row. All remained standing until everyone was inside and the doors were closed.

Speeches. About his zest for work, the power to improvise, dedication. Alice, the secretary, read a poem. Her hands trembled.

Hein spoke composed and formally about his successor, his face tight with pent-up sorrow. Someone from the employee-management council spoke on behalf of Molkenboer, who had no voice yet. A girl from the patients association told an anecdote in a whisper.

They are touched, she thought. They are frightened that death is so near. That no one escapes. Suddenly they've forgotten their rage and resentment and stand by Nico, as if there had been no fight. The need for reconciliation hangs above their heads like a suffocating cloud and obscures all annoyance and reproach. Their capacity for forgiveness makes them powerful. I don't forgive. I hope that that girl isn't here, that I don't have to see her. I hate him and I love him, but they can't do that. They aren't able to be powerless, they even have to fit death into their declarations and strategies. Their need to make a story is so great that they can't dwell on the content of the individual words. There has to be coherence. I am shards, I am splinters.

A man with a shaved head climbed on the podium.

"Erik Gerritsma," whispered Ineke, "the orderly from the burned pavilion."

Erik beckoned to the sides of the hall from where dozens of people started walking forward. They arranged themselves in rows on the platform, around the coffin, and looked ahead seriously. A man with curly hair, dressed in a black turtleneck, moved to stand in front of the group and hummed a note.

Then he lifted his hands and a song sounded. Two melodies spiraled around each other, moved apart, came back together, held each other in balance.

"Joy and pain...," she heard. "... Ever be mine, adieu, I say adieu ... we have to part..."

The singers' clothes were grubby. Some held hands, some cried unashamedly, others looked shy and barely dared to move their lips. Patients, she thought, the patients' choir. They are confused too, just like me, just like him. They are saying goodbye. They are sad. They are powerless, they have only their song.

Albert thanked those present on her behalf. Six men, Erik among them, carried the coffin in a slow procession over the sandy path. She heard the muffled footsteps of the crowd behind her. A blackbird sang in the top of a pine. No one talked.

The bearers left the path and walked over the mossy ground to the open grave. The hole was in the middle of an open spot on the slope of the dune, in the sun. She pushed her heels deep into the moss and watched how the men let the coffin drop into the ground. The sandy ground. With heads bent, people stood in a half circle around the grave. Albert said a last word. Then it was quiet.

Ineke took her gently by the arm and turned her a quarter turn. She disengaged her heels. Next to the grave was a pile of sand with a silver shovel standing up straight in the middle.

"You have to start, Louise."

She let her glance slide past the heads; in the last row she saw the friendly face of Sergeant Lantzaad. He held his cap clasped in front of his chest. She kneeled. Through the wood of black legs she could look down the slope of the dune. It seemed as if below, in the distance, a girl with short, red hair and a dull gray sweater was leaning against a tree. Her raised, white face was focused on the grave with great attention.

She ignored the shovel and stuck both hands deep into the sand. Then she unbent her knees and straightened her back. A pile of moist sand lay in her palms. She broke away from the bystanders, took a step forward, and let the sand fall with a dull thud on the coffin.

About the Author

Anna Enquist

Anna Enquist, a psychoanalyst and classically trained musician, was born in 1945. She began to write poetry in 1990, as she said, "from one day to the next." Today, she is one of the Netherlands' best-selling novelists, with a large readership in Germany, Austria, Switzerland, France, Italy and Sweden.

The fonts used in this book are from the Garamond family

Other works by Anna Enquist
available from *The* Toby Press

The Masterpiece
The Secret
The Injury